No More Heroes

The Teesside Crime Series

A. S. French

Neonoir Books

Also by A. S. French

Crime Fiction and Thrillers

The Astrid Snow series

Don't Fear the Reaper

The Killing Moon

Lost in America

Gone to Texas

The Final Girl

Snowstorm: An Astrid Snow Collection

The Ophelia Red series

Ophelia Red

The Detective Jen Flowers series

The Hashtag Killer

Serial Killer

Night Killer

The Killer Inside Them

The Frank Walker series

Where The Bodies Are Buried

Bodies of Evidence

Crime Short Stories

Crime Stories: A Collection

Call Me: An Astrid Snow Short Story

Writing as Andrew S. French

Science Fiction

The Time Traveller's Murder

The Mercy Sleep

Bodies

Another Girl, Another Planet

The Thief of Time Trilogy

The Queens of Heaven

The Queens of Time

The Queens of Space

The Arcane Supernatural Thriller Series

The Arcane

The Arcane Identity

The Arcane Quest

The Arcane Ultimatum

The Ella Finn Fantasy Novella Series

Ella and the Elementals

Ella and the Multiverse

Ella and the Monsters

Ella and the Dreamers

Supernatural Short Stories

Dead Souls

Dead Souls II

The Shadow

Go to www.andrewsfrench.com for more information.

Chapter 1

The Charm

It was a warm day to die.

The sun sank into the sea like a massive overcooked egg. The air had lost its late summer haze, replaced with the chill of the approaching night. An aroma of saltwater drifted over from below the cliffs. A grey-haired man watched the light turning into dusk, feeling the wind on his cheeks and listening to the gulls chattering above him. His neck ached as he glanced up at them, sensing their accusations hovering near his head like the sword of Damocles.

And he had a lot to answer for.

He stood beside an impressive sculpture of a giant steel bracelet with ten individual charms. The artwork's official name was the Circle, but the locals knew it as the Charm Bracelet. The charms seemed to gaze at him as if they were wondering why he was there, so far from his comfort zone. The moggie, in particular, appeared to be judging him, resurrecting a memory of a family feline that had died when the man's son was a young boy. A speeding car had struck the cat, leaving blood and guts all over the front garden as the poor animal had dragged its way home. The boy wept, but the man had offered no sympathy to his son.

'You must learn life's harsh lessons,' he'd told his only child.

The wind caressed his cheeks as he touched the rough metal of the design. In his youth, before becoming a man of science, he'd spent a lot of time reading fantastic fiction, dreaming of new worlds he could travel to and escape from his difficult life. Now, many years later, he imagined The Charm as a portal to one of those impossible places, somewhere he could disappear and forget about the painful decision he had to make. Still, whatever he decided, it would devastate those close to him.

The Charm overlooked the sea, far enough from the cliff edge so he recognised there was no danger of him being blown into the choppy waters a hundred feet below. Yet, he also knew this stretch of the Cleveland Way was notorious as a place where lost souls had felt there was nothing left for them in life but to embrace the waves beneath them. All along the route, memorials had been placed by grieving parents, family and friends. He'd read the cards on his way there, words of hope and encouragement to those who might visit those cliffs with only one thought: to hurl themselves into the cold water at the bottom.

The walk had been challenging, his knees creaking as he struggled up the cliff and scuffing his shoes through the dirt. His breathing had dribbled out in short bursts, resembling his father and his lifetime of smoking forty cigarettes a day. Long ago, as a young lad, he'd cycled up the hill to get to the cliffs, continuing along narrow edges, carrying his bike over his shoulder and down into the nearby fishing village. But that had been in another life, long before The Charm, and when he'd been full of ambition and arrogance.

It had driven him into medicine, that combination of desire and conceit, creating barriers between him and those he loved.

But not anymore. He'd finally admitted to his mistakes and was ready to apologise to those he'd hurt. Looking at the impressive sculpture, he understood how human connections had always constrained him. The bracelet stood on its edge with ten charms suspended from the top. Each was a three-dimensional image representing a story of local culture, tradition, or folklore. He'd visited it many times, but knew the debate continued regarding which tales they represented. Constructed in neighbouring Skinningrove, each piece was made from locally produced metals. The sculptor, Richard Farrington, had lived nearby in Skelton village and had included, amongst others, three-dimensional representations of a cat, horse, starfish, and even a mermaid. Described by Farrington as a 'giant charm bracelet', it had become a local landmark. Then, in 1996, somebody used specialised tools to saw through the work at its base and rolled the sculpture into the sea. Only the figure of a horse was recovered. Farrington's new circle, a replica of the first, had witnessed a Midsummer Day wedding, was the subject of stories by a local writers' group and, according to an urban legend, was a place where dark magic and superstition came together.

The Charm had endured for over thirty years, withstanding everything nature had thrown at it: wind, rain, sleet, and even several more attempts of vandalism by disaffected youths. He thought of its survival through the harshest regimes as he touched the mermaid, feeling a connection with the sculpture he hadn't before. Like it, he'd survived the slings and arrows of ignorance and jealousy and had weathered the emotional storms of those around him. He placed one hand on his beating heart, took a deep breath to inhale the countryside and the sea, and felt more alive than at any other time in his life.

His euphoria masked him from the blow that struck his shoulder. A gull screeched as the old man's legs gave way, his knee cracking and sending a stab of electricity through his body. His head bounced off the Charm, catching the edge of the cat before he crashed into the ground. Grass and dirt leapt into the air, scrambling into his mouth and eyes. He lifted one hand to his throat to stop the choking, spitting debris into the earth. Insects crawled over his wrinkled hands as a spider scuttled over his wrist and up his sleeve to disappear inside his clothes. The ringing in his ears sent shooting pain through his skull, but he still heard the footsteps around him.

'What...?'

It was all he said before he blacked out.

Chapter 2

The Visit

Teo Andreescu had a tough task to do, and she wasn't looking forward to it. She scratched at her leg, struggling to adjust to her new trousers and realising her waist wasn't as slim as she'd assumed. She took a deep breath and resisted the temptation to get the chocolate bar in her pocket.

Her discomfort was made worse by the oppressive temperature in the car. The heat was unbearable, resulting from one of those summer days scientists had said everybody would have to get used to in Britain. She opened the windows and increased the radio's volume. Billy Idol's "Hot in the City" blared out of the speakers, and she knew God was playing tricks on her. Not that she believed in a Divine Being. Her parents, who hadn't spoken to each other since their divorce, were not religious. Still, Teo's grandfather was a devout Christian from his strict upbringing before fleeing Romania as a refugee at the end of World War II. Growing up, she'd spent many hours listening to his stories of how God had saved him from the ravages of tyranny, but none of it had changed her perception that religion was nothing but a crutch for fear of death. Not that death didn't concern her, it would be impossible not to in her job, but at twenty-three, she understood that barring serious ill health or an accident, it would be a long time before she'd have to worry about her mortality.

She drove through a wooded area, smiling as the scenery lifted her heart. Bright reds, yellows, and greens surrounded her, making Teo feel like she was driving into a rainbow. She sucked in nature's heavy aromas through the open window, letting them revitalise her aching body. She'd been working twelve-hour shifts for ten days, and it was finally taking its toll. But she'd get a break once she delivered her message.

For her vacation, Teo considered returning to Whitby to visit her mother but thought better of it, knowing it would only increase her stress, thinking instead of heading somewhere well away from her parents. Maybe go up to Scotland and take in a gig or two. Edinburgh had some of her favourite small venues and clubs, places she'd visited several times, and they would be just what she needed to wash away her recent experiences of human depravity.

Her phone, which she'd placed on the empty passenger seat, vibrated with an incoming message. She glanced at the name on the screen, unsurprised to see who it was from, but still shocked the chief constable had given her such a task. As she recalled her meeting with him a few hours ago, the music changed on the radio to "Karma Police" by Radiohead and drifted through the car, and she knew some invisible force was messing with her.

But it was no god, only the coincidence of synchronicity.

The phone buzzed again as she peered at the building ahead, a magnificent structure built during Queen Victoria's reign. She hoped the insides had undergone an upgrade and renovation for the sake of the person she was on her way to visit. It was perpendicular, with four floors containing offices, residential rooms, admin facilities, recreation quarters, secure units, a large kitchen, toilets and showers. She knew all this because she'd checked the hospital's website before setting off on her mission.

She parked at the front of the building and looked at her phone. The text message from Chief Constable Beckett was brief.

Call me as soon as you leave Redlands.

Teo didn't reply, stepping out of the car and peering at the entrance to Redlands Park Hospital.

Redlands.

That was its official title, her local NHS psychiatric unit, but she knew that wasn't what some locals called it.

Bedlam.

It was a name with a long history.

Bedlam: Bethlem Royal Hospital, the first asylum for the mentally ill in England, was a word that would be used generically for all psychiatric hospitals and sometimes colloquially for an uproar. In 1247, the asylum was founded at Bishopsgate, just outside the London wall; it was then known as the Priory of St. Mary of Bethlehem, from which the variant spellings Bedlam and Bethlem sprang. In 1547, it was granted by Henry VIII to the City of London as a hospital for the mentally ill. It subsequently became infamous for the brutal treatment meted out to its patients. Bedlam was open to fee-paying spectators in the 17th and 18th centuries, but this disruptive practice ended in 1770. Teo watched the gulls fly overhead and wondered if anyone would treat those inside Redlands as exhibits to be gawked at. Then she thought about who she was on her way to see there.

Her phone rang as she exited the car and approached the entrance, stopping to answer the call.

'I'm at work, Mum.'

The interruption irritated Teo. She scratched at her free hand before lifting it to bite her nails.

'It won't take long, Teodora.'

Her parents were the only ones who called Teo by her full name. She moved away from the people staring at her and into the shadows. She dug a fingernail into her skin and drew blood. She placed it on her lips and sucked on it, enjoying the taste.

'What's so important, Mum?'

'I'm struggling with the salon, Teodora. The increases in the electricity and gas bills have crippled me.' Teo pressed the phone to her ear. 'The landlord is threatening to kick me out if I don't pay.'

'I don't think they can legally do that, Mum. Is that why you called, so I can check that?' It wouldn't be the first time one of her parents had asked her to use her job to help them with something.

There was a long sigh down the phone before her mother spoke. 'No, Teodora, that's not why I'm calling.'

Teo was leaning against the wall next to an open window where she could see inside Redlands. A group was sitting around a table and talking, but she couldn't hear them. Half had their backs to her, and she wondered if one of them was the person she was there to see.

She lowered her voice. 'So, what do you want, Mum?'

Her mother's tone rose enough to make the phone vibrate against Teo's cheek. 'I thought you might lend me the money your grandfather left you.'

Before she replied, her mobile pinged with a new message.

Have you spoken to the doctors yet?

'I'll ring you later, Mum. I'm working.'

Teo ended the call before her mother could reply, and she answered the chief constable.

I'm just heading into Redlands, sir.

Good. Call me as soon as you leave there. I want to know how he reacts to the bad news.

She put her phone away, strode up the steps, and stepped inside. Upon entering Redlands, metal banging against metal assaulted her senses. She grimaced and placed her hands over her ears, moving to the reception and showing the woman her warrant card.

'Sorry about the noise,' the receptionist, name-tagged as Emma, said. 'We're having an extension built onto the kitchen. How can I help you, Detective Sergeant Andreescu?'

'I'm here to see a patient. Erasmus Bukowski.'

Emma's eyes sparkled. 'Oh, the Inspector. Everybody loves him here.' She came out from behind the plastic screen. 'You're the first visitor he's ever had.' She nodded towards another door. 'He's probably in the lounge now. He does like his afternoon game of Bridge. I'll take you to Dr Ramone.'

'Dr Ramone?'

'Yes,' Emma said. 'You need his permission before speaking to any of our residents. I'm sure it will be fine.'

Teo didn't argue, following her through the building, thinking of the Ramones singing "Baby I Love You" as they went. They strode past the kitchen, her nostrils mugged by the stench of cafeteria food reminiscent of the crap she had to eat at school. The screech of a drill made her wince. The odour of fried chicken created invisible fingers clutching at the insides of her stomach. She couldn't remember the last time she'd eaten. Voices rebounded off the walls in the corridor before Emma took her around a corner to Dr Ramone's office. The receptionist knocked and waited for the command to enter. She opened the door when it came, ushering Teo inside and making the introductions. Then she left the two of them, and Teo told him who she was there to see.

He spoke through teeth so white she assumed he was American.

'We don't get many official visitors here, and I believe you must be Erasmus's first since he joined us a year ago.'

She nodded. 'Can I see him?'

Dr Ramone got up from behind his desk. 'Let's go for a walk. I'll give you a tour of the unit.'

She was surprised but didn't argue, being in no rush to see Bukowski and tell him the bad news. Instead, Teo followed the doctor out, smelling a mixture of antiseptic and deodorant coming from him. His expression was unmoving, with thin lips and a sharp nose under brown eyes. They moved down the corridor before Ramone stopped.

'The large room is the lounge. Right behind it is the arts and crafts area. Creative therapy takes place there. Of course, there are other types of treatment, too.' He pointed to a door near the far corner. 'And that's the entrance to the gym.'

Teo controlled her surprise. 'You have a gym?'

Ramone nodded. 'It's always supervised to ensure residents don't hurt themselves or others, but exercise can be an essential mode of therapy.' Teo pushed at her mouth so it wasn't in the shape of a large O anymore. 'They didn't have any exercise equipment at my previous employment. The manager thought it was too dangerous, so I allowed some residents to run through the facility to burn off their excess energy. It turned into the Forest Gump Olympics at times.'

She couldn't tell if he was joking or not. 'By residents, you mean patients?'

His expression finally changed, revealing a slug-like smile. 'We prefer the term resident.'

'Does Detective Inspector Bukowski use the gym?'

He scrutinised her as he shoved both hands into his jacket pockets. 'Is he still employed by Cleveland Police? I assumed he might have left the force when he joined us here.'

She shook her head. 'The chief constable gave DI Bukowski special dispensation to take as much time as he wanted off work.'

Ramone moved closer to her. 'Are you aware of the incident that led to his voluntary admission here?'

'I am, but I thought DI Bukowski's condition was something he'd had since childhood?'

He removed a hand from his pocket, and she noticed the edge of a tattoo on his wrist.

'That's true, DS Andreescu. Unfortunately, when Inspector Bukowski was a child in the '80s and '90s, the awareness of neurodiversity and its treatments were not as progressive as they are now. If it had been diagnosed earlier, he might have had a quite different life.'

'Neurodiversity?'

'Yes. Neurodiversity is the idea that it's normal and acceptable for people to have brains that function differently from one another. Rather than thinking something is wrong or problematic when some folks don't operate similarly to others, neurodiversity embraces all differences. The concept of neurodiversity recognises that brain function and behavioural traits are simply indicators of how diverse the human population is.'

'So, it's not all about pumping him so full of drugs that he'll feel like he's underwater?'

He frowned at her. 'From your tone, Sergeant, should I assume you've had a negative experience with the medical profession's treatment of psychiatric disorders?'

She didn't answer. 'Can I see him now?'

His stone face returned. 'That depends. Erasmus has progressed considerably in the last year, and I wouldn't anything to set him back. So why are you here?'

Teo repeated what Chief Inspector Beckett had relayed to her a few hours ago. 'I'll give him the information, or you can.'

Dr Ramone didn't hesitate. 'I'll take you straight to him.'

She nodded, preparing to deliver the worst possible news to a fellow police officer she'd never met.

Chapter 3

The Hospital

Erasmus Bukowski enjoyed his morning. The shower had warmed his skin as the bouquet of fresh strawberries from the shampoo revitalised his mind. By the time he'd dressed, he was already listening to David Bowie's *Hunky Dory* in his head.

When he strolled into the dining area, he saw that the kitchen staff had replaced the bottle of brown sauce he'd thrown against the wall yesterday. Bridget, the nurse, had brushed against his hand, setting off his OCD of being touched, and, in his rage, Erasmus hurled the container as far away as possible. The plastic had shattered, spreading brown liquid across the surface as if there had been a visit from an elephant suffering from explosive diarrhoea.

In his early days at Redlands, such behaviour would have seen him removed to his room. However, the staff and residents now understood that his actions weren't from malice, but an involuntary reaction caused by the unusual wiring in his brain. And he'd cleaned up the mess and apologised to everyone as soon as it had happened.

But today was a good day for personal contact, and he

felt much more tactile. The breakfast had been his favourite: sausages, bacon, black pudding, eggs and toast. The vegans and vegetarians scowled at him, but it was only good-natured ribbing. Everybody at Redlands accepted and respected other's beliefs and principles beyond a few minor disagreements once in a while. It was a breath of fresh air for Erasmus, who'd been brought up in a household simmering with family tensions that either went unsaid or exploded in verbal violence.

After breakfast, he spent an hour in the gym, listening through his headphones to Florence & the Machine while he rode on the exercise bike, imagining he was climbing one of the steepest hills on the Tour de France. Cycling through the countryside or along the coast from Redcar to Whitby was among the few things he missed about the outside world.

Erasmus's medication made him restless, creating the need to move endlessly. The TV in the lounge was muted, but the flickering images of a Tom and Jerry cartoon spread across the digital screen. He gazed at the bright colours and manic scenes as the cat tried to kill the mouse with over-sized weapons. The activity reminded him of an incident with his father when he was seven or eight of, his dad smashing a porcelain pot into smithereens as his anger erupted out of nothing. His mother was shopping, and his father was not at work for unspecified reasons. Erasmus had been too young to understand how stressful a hospital doctor's life could be, but this traumatic event was the first time he witnessed the fury of his father's unbridled rage. Unfortunately, it wouldn't be the last.

He carried his journal, phone, headphones, and the latest novel he was reading, Douglas Stuart's *Shuggie Bain*. He tasted toothpaste at the back of his mouth and smelt the familiar aroma of lavender hairspray approaching him. He turned to see the broad smile of Alexa Cromer lighting up the room.

She pointed at the book. 'That will break your heart, Razzie.' She was the only person who called him that. 'You should read a cheerful author, like Hubert Selby Jr or Hunter S. Thompson.'

He waved his journal at her. 'I'm writing my own. It's called *Fear and Loathing in Teesside*.'

She sidled up to him, reaching to grab his arm before stopping. 'Is this a touching or no touching day?'

He smiled at her. 'You kept my list?'

She returned his grin and took a piece of folded A4 paper from the back pocket of her faded jeans.

'Sure,' Alexa waved it at him. 'How to prevent triggering Erasmus's instability. Do you want me to recite all twelve suggestions?'

He shook his head. 'No, I can remember them. And I'm fine with personal contact today.'

She beamed at him and weaved her arm through his. 'Great. So, this book of yours – am I in it?'

They walked towards the table near the window where two other residents played chess. 'Do you want to be in it?'

She stopped pulling on him and rolled her tongue between her lips.

'I'm not sure. Would I be a glamorous, super intelligent female spy ass-kicking my way around the world while seducing a bevvy of supermodels and Hollywood actresses?'

He nodded. 'Of course – strictly all true to life.'

When Erasmus had voluntarily entered Redlands a year ago, Alexa was already in the facility. She was the one who introduced him to the other residents and gave him a tour of the building. She also calmed him down during those early days of his most manic moods, helping him as much as the medication did. He smiled as he thought of the drugs, knowing he was close to coming off them. Of course, there would still be a long way to go before he felt comfortable returning to the outside world – he'd calculated another twelve months at least – but it would be good to lose that chemical dependence.

She beamed at him. 'That's great, Razzie. Then we can escape here together.'

'Are you ready to return to the outside world, Alexa?'

She let go of him and shrugged. 'Maybe. I need to speak to Dr Ramone about my therapy.' She glanced at the clock on the wall. 'Shit! I'm late to see him.' She ran out of the room without another word.

He watched her leave as a former MI5 operative approached him. At least, that's what Barry claimed to be.

'You coppers have it easy,' Barry said to Erasmus as they sat at the table. They drank orange juice while everybody else enjoyed a game show on the big screen TV.

Erasmus slurped his drink. 'How come, Agent Styles?'

Barry removed his reading glasses and pushed aside yesterday's copy of the *Financial Times*.

'Well, unless there's a riot or an ongoing major terrorist incident, you only have to deal with the odd burglar or teenager nicked for having a few cannabis joints hidden in his underpants. MI5's mission is to keep the country safe from domestic threats, and most of the time, the public doesn't realise how dangerous those are.'

After meeting Barry for the first time, it hadn't taken Erasmus long to understand that the other man got most of his information from Bond movies and spy novels. But at least he was never dull. Though, at times, Erasmus knew that dullness would help ease his overstimulated mind.

'Recorded crime is at a twenty-year high, Barry, with over two million violent crimes reported against people last year. All this while the police have had to deal with severe cuts, including losing nearly 25,000 support staff and 22,000 officers in the last thirteen years.'

Barry shrugged. 'What do you expect from successive Tory governments?'

Erasmus knew that was Barry's attempt to get him to talk about politics, but he wasn't going down that rabbit hole, understanding it would set off one of his episodes.

'Why did you leave MI5?'

The big man laughed. 'Who said I did, Inspector? Perhaps I'm in Redlands undercover, seeking out threats to our national security.'

'*All the President's Men*,' somebody shouted at the quiz on the TV.

Martin, a secondary school teacher, joined them. His partner had died in a car accident six months before, and his world had unravelled rapidly after that tragedy.

'Why do blokes always judge themselves and others by their job or lack of one?'

Barry shook his head. 'What else is important in life, Marty?'

Martin sighed. 'You need to improve your communication skills, mate. Not everything is based on competitive banter, trying to prove who has the best profession or career or the most money.'

Barry grinned. 'What's that old saying? Those who can do, those who can't, teach.'

'So, who taught you to be a spy, Bazza? Austin Powers?'

Erasmus stepped between them. 'Speaking of competition, we need one more for Bridge.'

'Sure,' Martin said. 'As long as I'm not partnered with Jimmy Bond.'

'Nine Inch Nails,' a red-headed woman shouted at the TV. Her name was Laura, and Erasmus knew she was an excellent card player.

'Do you want to partner with Barry at Bridge, Laura?' Erasmus asked as he approached her.

She twisted her head from side to side, moving her lips to the music accompanying an advert on the screen. Erasmus recognised it as Joy Division's "Love Will Tear Us Apart." He glanced at the TV, seeing an old couple trying to sell funeral services to the audience.

'Anything for you, Inspector,' she said.

He got the pack of cards, and the four sat at the table near the window that looked onto the North Sea. He dealt, and Laura opened her mouth. He knew what was coming next and didn't mind. Dr Ramone and his colleagues encouraged every resident to communicate and express their feelings with others as much as possible. As long as the person felt comfortable talking – or listening – he said it would help understand why the human brain sometimes seemed to reject the perceived way of thinking. Ramone called it "the messy bits of people's lives" we occasionally struggled to comprehend without getting upset.

Erasmus sorted his cards as Laura told them about her previous life as a writer of children's books. Then, they played Bridge, which had always helped Erasmus sort his mind into order from chaos. The conversation flowed as they spoke about drinking too much, not eating the right food, being fed up with work, enjoying work, worrying about death, worrying about living, suffering from depression, negotiating bisexuality, difficulties with partners, anxieties about children, joys of partners and children, and so on.

'I think my last book was the best I've ever written,' Laura said as she trumped Erasmus's ace of spades. 'Much better than anything from one of those celebrity authors.'

Barry laughed. 'Yeah, I read the copy you brought with you here. What's it called again?'

Erasmus had also read the book created for children ages five to ten. '*Porker Pig Goes to Prison.*'

Martin shook his head. 'How did your publisher not realise all the animal characters were caricatures of politicians?'

Laura scooped up all her winning cards while Erasmus added the score to the running total, not that there was much for him and Martin.

'Who's to say they didn't?' she replied.

All four laughed together, even though Erasmus knew Laura's condition had worsened when she produced that book. She told him several times about how her mania was consuming her then, her lack of sleep, staying awake for days so she could finish the project. He understood how she felt, recognising how euphoric highs could make you feel as if everything was possible and drive the creative urge to the point it might overwhelm the mind. When it happened to him, it was the most incredible feeling ever, better than sex, booze, or drugs. There was nothing to compare to it.

But then came the lows. And he realised no high was worth those.

'I heard you're working on a new book while holidaying in Redlands, Laura,' Barry said.

She smiled as she dealt. 'Yeah, and I'm using all of you as characters in it. So, no suing me when it's published.'

Erasmus sorted his cards, counting the points and realising he had a decent hand for once. 'I hope you've given us cute names, Laura.'

She nodded. 'Of course, boys. Bazza is Doofus, the Bear; Martin is a kangaroo called Garoo, and you, my dear Bukowski, are Inspector Bu, the leader of a crime-fighting group of animals trying to put a confused world right again. There are all kinds of shenanigans as you combat the following: climate change, corrupt governments, and dark media influences.'

'And who are you in this?' Erasmus said.

She grinned at him. 'Why, I'm the femme fatale of the piece, the enigmatic Laura Bacchanal.'

Barry shook his head. 'And this is aimed at children?'

'You've got to catch them young, Bazza,' she said. 'Why do you think our glorious leaders are so desperate to construct the school curriculum into something that manipulates fledgling minds to be unthinking and uncritical of the rich and privileged?'

They had been playing for two hours when a nurse approached the table.

'You have a visitor, Erasmus. A police officer.'

He put down his winning hand and got up, wondering who had died.

Chapter 4

The Assessment

One year ago.

A man in a crumpled suit and two in white uniforms sat opposite Erasmus. The room was stuffy, like being inside a microwave dropped into a volcano. He pulled at the collar of the cheap gown the hospital had provided, trying to ignore the dryness in his mouth. His testicles had shrivelled up in the heat, resembling an emaciated chicken, and he had a nightmare of the gown drooping off, so he sat there naked before them.

'When do I get my clothes back?'

'Soon,' the crumpled suit said. 'I'm Dr Ramone, the head of this facility, and these are my colleagues Dr Cafferty and Dr Nish.'

Cafferty had a scar on his chin and a look in his eyes straight from the hard streets of Glasgow. Nish flourished a disconcerting moustache reminiscent of a dead caterpillar

Erasmus had wiped from his kitchen window some years back.

He twitched in his gown, the cheap material irritating his skin, his hand trembling as he resisted the urge to scratch his balls.

'The Crucial Three.'

'What?' Dr Ramone said.

Erasmus shook his head. 'Nothing. Just a personal joke.'

'What brings you to the hospital?' Dr Ramone said.

Erasmus wished he'd brought his journal with him. 'I have bipolar disorder, and I'm in a rapidly evolving, acute mixed state with psychotic features.'

Dr Cafferty removed a notebook from his uniform. 'When were you diagnosed as bipolar?'

Erasmus crossed his legs, watching the gown expose the large scar under his left knee, a remnant of a schoolyard fight when he was fourteen. Three of them had jumped on him on the school field but regretted it soon after.

'It was the day I took my mother to the care home for her dementia four years ago.' The doctors looked at each other. 'My GP sent me to a specialist at Cleveland Hospital.'

'There are several types of bipolar and related disorders,' Dr Ramone said. 'With bipolar I disorder, you've had at least one manic episode that may be preceded or followed by hypomanic or major depressive episodes. Sometimes, mania may trigger a break from reality, what we call psychosis.

'Then there is bipolar II disorder. Here, you've had at least one major depressive episode and at least one hypomanic episode, which is less extreme than mania, but you've never had a manic episode.

'Finally, there's cyclothymic disorder. You've had at

least two years — or one year in children and teenagers — of many periods of hypomania symptoms and periods of depressive symptoms, though less severe than major depression.' He glanced through his notes. 'We don't appear to have the details of your diagnosis, Mr Bukowski.'

He didn't feel like smiling, but did, anyway.

'Please, call me Erasmus. I have bipolar II disorder.'

Dr Ramone nodded. 'Bipolar II disorder is not a milder form of bipolar I disorder, but a separate diagnosis. While the manic episodes of bipolar I disorder can be severe and dangerous, individuals with bipolar II disorder can be depressed for more extended periods, which can cause significant impairment. Does that sound like what's been happening to you, Erasmus?'

'Yes. I guess I've been like this all my life, but I've been able to live and work with no major incidents until recently. That's why I came here.'

Cafferty scribbled something into his notebook. 'Okay, Mr Bukowski. Can you tell us what's happening inside your head?'

Erasmus scratched above the scar, the phantom pain returning with a vengeance and shooting up his thigh. He gritted his teeth and did his best to ignore the throbbing in his leg.

'Aren't *you* the ones supposed to tell *me* what's happening inside my head?'

Dr Ramone gazed into his eyes. 'Can you explain how you've been feeling?'

Erasmus sighed. 'I've been fine for a while, with only a few minor episodes I could control, until recently when everything has felt like a rollercoaster; manic highs rapidly followed by subterranean lows. My emotions change with lightning speed and are unpredictable. I have no control.

There are auditory and visual hallucinations, voices in my head, and uncontrollable OCD. Coming here is my last hope.'

Ramone reached behind his chair and retrieved a computer tablet, brushing his fingers across the screen.

'That sounds more like Bipolar I disorder, Erasmus.'

Erasmus shrugged. 'You're the experts.'

Dr Nish cleared his throat. 'Can you be more specific about how your mania has manifested?'

'Sure,' Erasmus said. 'I have endless energy and confidence, with little need for sleep. I'm an atheist, but I hear God whispering in my ear, telling me how special I am. I'm a moth, fluttering between an infinite choice of shimmering lightbulbs. My eyes become frog-like, my nose twitches like that woman in the TV show about witchcraft, while every hair along my arms jumps to attention. Everything around me is heightened; the light is brighter, or the dark turns impenetrable. The slightest sound fills my head as if Motörhead and Metallica are playing inside my skull. My taste buds throb as food and drink arrive straight from hell or heaven. Sex is the greatest thing ever until it's over, and a void replaces my heart. I see colours everywhere: vivid reds, yellows, and blues lingering in the air like the spirits of long-lost family and friends. I go on spending sprees online, buying dozens of books I'll never read, CDs I won't listen to, and DVDs that will never leave their cases. They get stored with all the others as I crave things to collect.' He took a deep breath. 'Then the downside arrives. Most of the time is spent in bed, though it's impossible to sleep. So many thoughts infect my brain they threaten to overwhelm me. I think of all the mistakes I've made in my life, of the people I've let down or disappointed. I remember those crime victims I could never get justice for and the criminals who laughed at me when they walked free from court. Only they didn't walk; they strutted. Depression usually follows as the elevated mood ebbs away. Then I have no energy, possessed of listlessness, wanting nothing but endless sleep. My self-worth is non-existent, and I cannot concentrate on the simplest of things; easily irritated and restless.'

He scratched his knee, digging his nails into the skin until the blood trickled out. He let it drip onto the floor and watched the three doctors making their notes. None of them seemed to notice what he'd done.

'How long have you been a police officer, Erasmus?' Dr Ramone said.

'Twenty-one years, joining when I was nineteen.'

'Has your neurodiversity ever impacted or interfered with your work?' Dr Nish asked.

Erasmus crossed his arms. 'No.'

Dr Ramone scrutinised him. 'That's not what you told our staff when you arrived here last night.'

Erasmus watched his blood settle into a small pool on the floor.

'Yes, I'm sorry.' His shoulders slumped. 'I was King of the World, Kong bounding up the Empire State Building. Not to escape from those pursuing me, but to chase down all the criminals I knew were out there. There was no Fay Wray in my hand, only the names of killers, muggers, and rapists I was about to bring to justice. Lack of evidence meant little to me, knowing I'd find it eventually. And if I didn't? Well, there were always ways around that. Following police procedure was as likely as me following the Yellow Brick Road. I became my own judge and jury, ready to right the world's wrongs with whatever it took.

'My mind was on fast forward. I thought it was because of the case I was involved in - a missing child - and my brain was racing through every possibility. I collected copies of all the witness statements and took them home. There must have been thirty, which I organised chronologically from when the witnesses had last seen the young girl. They were laid on my carpet, where I stared at them for hours, waiting for a clue to jump out. When that didn't happen, I grabbed a pair of scissors and cut them into individual pieces, rearranging those as if I were David Bowie cutting up song lyrics to make new tunes.

'Then came the FALL. I tumbled from the great height my mood had elevated me to, crashing down and hitting every obstacle on the way. I forgot to read a suspect his rights, meaning he walked free from court. He was drunk two weeks later when he drove his car into a woman on a zebra crossing. He died, and she'll never walk again.' He lowered his head as he spoke. 'And we never found that missing girl.'

Rafferty made another note. 'The lows and highs you feel, and the other symptoms, have you had them for a long time?'

Erasmus dug his nails into his palms. 'Since I was a child.'

'The hallucinations and the voices?'

Erasmus shook his head. 'No. They're recent.'

It was only a little lie that he didn't think was too important. It didn't matter what had happened to him before, only what he felt now.

'Before coming here,' Dr Ramone said, 'have you had any therapy or medication for your condition?'

The laughter trickled out of Erasmus. 'Does cigarettes and alcohol count as medication? Or casual sex as therapy?'

Rafferty wrote furiously in his book as Ramone replied.

'Are you willing to accept our recommendations regarding therapy and medication for you?'

Erasmus glanced at the bare walls that reminded him of a dodgy Geordie nightclub he frequented. 'That's why I'm here.'

The doctors pushed their heads together, speaking words he couldn't hear before Dr Ramone turned to him.

'We'll get you settled into a room and begin group therapy tomorrow. How does that sound, Erasmus?'

As Erasmus replied, Bowie was singing about a couple of kooks in his head.

'Perfect.'

Chapter 5

The Revelation

Dr Ramone's mobile phone vibrated as he led Teo down the corridor. He looked at the screen as they stood outside a room.

'Redlands has twenty-four rooms for residents and does not specialise in any specific mental health condition or age group.'

She wondered why he'd told her that. 'In other words, there's a wide diversity of neurodiversity.'

He smiled at her. 'Indeed. And I have a therapy session to attend right now.' Ramone pushed the door open. 'Erasmus should be here soon. I wouldn't normally leave a visitor alone in the building, but with you being a police officer, I guess it's okay. As long as you're fine with that?'

She nodded. 'I am.'

'Excellent. Erasmus will show you the way out once you've finished.'

He slipped the phone into his pocket and left. Teo stepped into the room, leaving the door open. It was sparse in furniture: a single bed, a small wooden nightstand, shelving for clothes, no coat hangers, and one lonely chair. Everything was bolted to the floor. The walls were bare, besides some marks in a few spots where pictures appeared missing. She wondered what used to hang there. Most of the space was occupied by books and magazines: Frank Herbert's *Dune* to Gail Honeyman's *Eleanor Oliphant is Completely Fine*; *The Complete Works of Shakespeare* to Darwin's *Origin of Species*, *Home and Gardens* to *Private Eye*. Teo ran her fingers over a glossy magazine before seeing the mobile phone near the bed.

The chief constable told me Bukowski wasn't allowed a phone in Redlands.

'I can only use it to listen to music.' She turned to see the man to whom she'd come to give the bad news. 'Residents aren't permitted the internet or to make phone calls without permission, but Dr Ramone allowed me to have the mobile because listening to music helps control my moods. But they removed the SIM card, and it's not connected to any network.'

Teo peered at him, someone she'd only seen in photographs before, Detective Inspector Erasmus Bukowski: six-foot tall, athletic physique, blue eyes, short dark hair. He was in his early forties yet looked ten years younger.

Regular therapy and exercise must have done him a world of good.

Then she wondered what medication he might be taking.

She showed him her warrant card. 'I'm Detective Sergeant Teo Andreescu.'

He stepped further into the room and dropped a notebook on the bed.

'Is Sam Beckett checking up on me?'

Teo didn't deny it. 'Chief Constable Beckett asked me to see you, sir.'

Bukowski shook his head. 'Call me, Erasmus. Where are you based, DS Andreescu?'

'Redcar.'

'You must be new there.'

She nodded. 'I joined just after you left, transferred from Whitby.'

'Whitby? That's a stunning location for chasing criminals. What made you leave there for here?'

Teo hadn't thought she'd go to Redlands to give Bukowski her life story, but at least it meant she didn't just turn up to deliver the bad news and bugger off.

'I was born in Whitby and moved here when I was seven in 2007 before returning to Whitby for my police training.'

'Straight out of uni?'

'Yes. I got a first-class degree in criminology from Teesside University.'

'Your parents must be very proud. I had plenty of qualifications when I became a copper twenty years ago, but I refused the opportunity of a place at Oxford to put on the blue uniform. My father wasn't happy about it.'

'My parents divorced and returned to Whitby.' She didn't know why she told him that. 'I'm unsure if they really understand why I wanted to become a police officer.'

Bukowski moved to his pile of books, and she watched him rearrange them from alphabetical order into genre. He held a paperback called *Mommie Dearest* as he spoke.

'Nobody knows the true version of ourselves, Teo – not even us. So, think how difficult it must be for our parents to understand our decisions.' She took a deep breath, ready to tell him why she was there. But then he picked up the notebook. 'I've kept journals for most of my life, and this is my latest one.'

'I had a diary as a teenager,' she said. That was until she stopped when her sadness filled all the pages.

He dropped the book onto the bed and clasped the journal to his chest.

'Bipolar disorder is probably the only illness where some believe there's an advantage to being unwell – this is the "creative myth." By harnessing the creative energy of a bipolar high, people can channel their mania for artistic purposes; they produce more and better writing, art, music, poetry, and other artistic endeavours. But people on a bipolar high are not on a creative high; they only think they are. They are full of great ideas, but before they can act on one, another comes along to push that genius thought aside. If I wrote a page daily for three months without the high, it would make more sense than trying to write a novel in three days during a manic phase.'

'You've spent your time here being creative?'

'A bit,' he said, opening the journal. 'Some people had invisible friends when they were kids, but I had an invisible rocket to fly around in. I used it to speed around the house and the garden, flying through school and irritating my teachers. But my brain was plugged into the rocket's engine, feeding off its fuel to fly through my exams and be top in all my classes. My father tried to dissuade me from joining the police, but I knew it was the only job for me. I was still inside that rocket when I cruised through my training and wore the uniform for the first time. Solving crimes and dealing with the seedier sides of life has helped me facilitate the mood swings, or at least they gave me excuses for why I had them. Police work isn't a regular job, so I always expected my reactions to it to be unusual: the joy of bringing a murderer to justice or helping victims find closure would create a manic high in my brain. On the other hand, was the opposite feeling of the lows brought about by the failures. And there were plenty of those. These were black pits of despair seemingly impossible to get out of. I assumed all coppers felt both of these highs and lows.'

He gazed at her, and she knew she couldn't put it off any longer.

'I'm here about your father, Dr James Bukowski.'

He closed his journal. 'Have you found him?'

She nodded. 'Yes.'

'Dead?'

'I'm afraid so.'

Teo waited for his emotions to show, for the tears or anger to come.

But he was unmoving. 'Where?'

'A couple walking their dog discovered his remains on the cliffs between Saltburn and Skinningrove.'

'The cliffs? My father was never a walker. I don't understand what he'd be doing up there.' He gripped the journal. 'Isn't it a local suicide spot?'

'Several people have jumped into the sea from there over the years,' she said. 'But that didn't happen with your father.'

'Was it an accident?'

The chief constable had given Teo strict instructions to tell Bukowski the bare minimum regarding what happened to his father, but she felt there were some things he deserved to know.

'Dr Toon hasn't completed her post-mortem yet, but it seems unlikely.'

Erasmus Bukowski suddenly looked older than he had done ten minutes ago.

'I'm surprised they got Bella for the autopsy.' He removed a pen from a desk drawer and wrote something in his journal. 'My father was one of her teachers during her medical studies.'

'Dr Bukowski was a surgeon?'

'Yes. Thirty years at Middlesbrough General and all the names it later acquired. It was his life, much more than his wife and child.' His eyelids flickered rapidly. 'Has anybody informed my mother?'

'I don't know, Erasmus. I was just told to come and give you the news.'

Darkness covered his face. 'I wonder if she still remembers him.' He sat on the bed. 'I took her to a care home on the day he disappeared. Her dementia had begun to overwhelm her.' He placed the journal under his pillow. 'Did Bella say when she thought my father died?'

'Dr Toon believes it was probably not long after he went missing.'

Erasmus's eyes brightened. 'So, he's either lain there for five years undiscovered, or somebody recently moved him to that location.'

'I don't know, Erasmus. I'm not part of the investigation.'

He looked at her as if just realising she was a police officer.

'Are you here to interview me about my father's death, DS Andreescu?'

She shook her head. 'No. I'm here to give you the news about your father, that's all.'

He got off the bed. 'Thank you for that, Teo. I'll show you out.'

She followed him from the room, retracing the route Dr Ramone had taken her.

'Do you intend to stay in Redlands much longer, Erasmus?'

They stopped near the reception desk. 'I'm unsure.' He smiled at her. 'Andreescu is of Romanian heritage, yes?'

Teo nodded. 'My grandparents came here from Transylvania as refugees after the Second World War.'

'And they lived in Whitby?'

She grinned. 'Yes. My grandfather told me it was because he read Stoker's book and thought a Romanian community would be living there. But, alas, he was to be disappointed.'

He returned her smile. 'My paternal grandfather, Leonard Bukowski, moved to the UK from Nazi Germany in 1939.'

'Have you ever visited Germany?'

'No. How about you with Romania?'

'Not yet, but one day I will. My grandfather told me so many stories about the place.'

She thought he'd start talking about holidays abroad, but then he changed tack.

'Do you enjoy working for Cleveland Police?'

The question surprised her, but she answered it honestly.

'I love the job, even though it's hard work and long hours. But I guess you already know that.'

'Did they ever find Amy Watson?'

The fatigue creeping up on Teo now threatened to consume her.

'No, I'm afraid not.'

Erasmus shook his head. 'How does an eight-year-old girl just vanish in the modern world of CCTV and camera phones everywhere?'

'The investigation is still ongoing.' She wanted to go home and sleep.

His shoulders slumped as he spoke. 'It took five years to find my father; he might have been out in the open all that time.'

'I'm sure the chief constable will keep you informed of the investigation, Erasmus.'

He stuck out his hand, and she shook it. 'I'm sure he will, Teo.'

She said goodbye and left Redlands, striding to her car before remembering she promised to call Sam Beckett. The chief constable had taken a shine to her as soon as she arrived at the station. 'You remind me of my oldest daughter,' he'd told her. Some of her colleagues weren't happy about that and were never slow to tell her, so it had caused several problems.

Teo took the phone from her jacket and called him.

'How did he take the news?' Beckett said as he answered the call.

'Well, I think, sir.'

'Did he ask any difficult questions about his father?'

'No.'

'Any emotional outbursts?'

'He took the news well.' Liquid lead seeped through her legs. 'Is there anything else, sir?'

'No; you did a good job, Teo. I've got another favour to ask you, but it can wait until tomorrow. You go home and get some rest.'

He ended the call, and she tried not to think about this other favour.

She drove away and wondered if she'd see Detective Inspector Erasmus Bukowski again.

Chapter 6

The First Day

One Year Ago

The unit buzzed with people, staff, and residents. Erasmus opened his journal and took notes, observing the name tags of the staff, writing brief descriptions of the residents: tall man with startling eyes; bald woman with trembling lips; thin bloke with arms covered in skull tattoos; a red-haired young woman winking at me; blue-eyed woman singing silent songs; a teenage boy reading *Lord of the Rings*; Idris Elba lookalike telling jokes to a pretty nurse.

'Are you spying on us?'

He closed the notebook, looking at the young woman gazing at him.

'No. My brain's on information overload, so I must write it all down to ease the stress in my head.'

She flashed him a wide smile. 'What's your name?'

'Erasmus.'

'I'm Alexa, you know, like the internet gadget. All you have to do is say my name and ask me a question, and I'll answer it or tell me to sing a song, and I'll be like Adele on happy pills. So go on, ask me a question.'

'How long have you been here?'

She frowned. 'Six months. Ask me a general knowledge question, something obscure, go on.'

He considered her request, digging into his memory for one of the few things he'd enjoyed with his father.

'Alexa, how many Marx Brothers were there?'

She beamed at him. 'There were five Marx Brothers, born in New York City between 1887 and 1901. They were boyhood vaudevillians with the stage names Chico, Harpo, Groucho, Gummo and Zeppo.'

Erasmus laughed. 'That's impressive.' He thought of another question. 'What was David Bowie's fifth album?'

She didn't hesitate. '*The Rise and Fall of Ziggy Stardust and the Spiders from Mars*, often shortened to *Ziggy Stardust*, is the fifth studio album by English musician David Bowie, released on 16 June 1972 in the United Kingdom through RCA Records.'

He shook his head. 'How do you do that?'

Alexa grinned at him. 'I have hyperthymesia, what people call perfect memory.' She glanced around the room. 'So, I remember everything I've ever read, which is great because it's so boring here.' She gripped his arm. 'What did you do before entering Redlands?'

'I'm a detective inspector in the police.'

'Wow, now that's impressive.' She dragged him to the wall. 'Tell me your history, Mr Inspector, and give me more things to memorise and stimulate my brain.'

'Why are you in here?'

Alexa let go of him. 'That's a bit personal. Why are you here? Did you kill a criminal?'

'I need to deal with my bipolar,' he said. 'Plus, I have OCD and anxiety issues.'

'Well, you're in the right place for all that.' She pointed at his journal. 'Is writing everything down one of your compulsions?'

He nodded. 'It started as a teenager, observing the world around me and recording it in minute detail.'

'That must have helped you as a copper.'

Erasmus agreed. 'It has its benefits.'

Dr Ramone entered the room with two white-uniformed nurses, a woman and a man. Alexa glanced at them.

'Have they put you on any meds yet?'

He shook his head. 'No.'

'Good.' She tapped her cheek. 'Don't let them give you drugs; they only worsen things. Find your remedies elsewhere.'

Erasmus opened the journal, writing as he spoke. 'Medication might be the only thing capable of maintaining my sanity.'

'That's crap,' Alexa said. 'What did people do before all these remedies Big Pharma pushes into us to make billions? I'll tell you what they did; they visited the local Wise Woman or healer and used natural herbs or physical exercise to alleviate their minds. That was before sadistic quacks and hacks appeared, cutting out bits of our brains, electrocuting us, or sticking leeches up our arses for entertainment. Then the drug barons had the bright idea to exploit the likes of us, filling us so full of chemicals it's any wonder the body and brain can work at all.' She waved at Dr Ramone as he walked around the room, talking to the residents. 'Thankfully, it's not like that here. They won't force drugs on you unless they think it's necessary and you agree, unlike some places I've been to.'

Her lips had moved at a thousand words a second, and Erasmus's fingers ached from writing it all down. But he'd had to do it, or she would have dazed his brain with a sensory overload.

'They were bad?'

Alexa's head bounced up and down on her shoulders like a nodding dog.

'Yeah, you're lucky you got into here, Inspector.'

'It was recommended to me as the best place in the area to help with mental illness.'

She screwed up her face and snorted at him. 'There's no such thing as mental illness – I'm just not adhering to society's behavioural norms. So, I had to come here to avoid the grief I was getting in the outside world.'

The sparkle in her eyes intrigued him. 'What happened to you?'

Alexa pursed her lips. 'I wore the wrong clothes and said the wrong things and annoyed all the wrong people who thought they were the right people, and I was upsetting the natural order of things.'

'The natural order of things?'

'You know, keeping women in their places, going back to traditional values – whatever they are – yadda, yadda, yadda, why aren't I having babies instead of singing punk rock songs?'

'You're in a band?'

That sparkle increased. 'I was before I came here. It's great to get up on stage and howl at the world.'

Erasmus opened his journal. 'I learnt to play the guitar as a kid and still write lyrics.'

'Maybe we should collaborate on some tunes.'

He closed the journal. 'Perhaps, but this is my first day here, and I hardly know you.'

Alexa crossed her arms. 'You think my comment about not behaving to societal norms means I've committed a criminal act, don't you, Inspector?'

Before he could answer, she turned from him and walked away. He smiled as she left. Redlands was more interesting than he thought it would be. The idea of returning to his old life was already a distant memory.

Chapter 7

The Station

Teo woke at six a.m. By six-thirty, she was jogging through the park near her flat. At six thirty-two, she increased her speed, sprinting across the grass, moving past the sculpture of local football legend Brian Clough, and heading for the lake at the bottom of the park. The wind caressed her hair, the barking dogs irritating her ears.

She reached the water in record time, her mind counting the seconds and minutes as easily as any clock, and turned to start another circuit. Her legs throbbed with the pleasure of exercise, her muscles warming to the day, when she saw a familiar group of three women running towards her. If she looked the other way and avoided their gaze, she wouldn't have to acknowledge their existence even though she'd known them since primary school. But she wasn't quick enough, and the tallest of the blondes, Sandra Hull, waved at her before the group stopped next to her. She could have gone around them, giving a hint of a smile, but she slammed on the brakes before stumbling headfirst into Hull's perfect body.

'Hey, Teo, fancy seeing you here.'

Teo didn't say she did that run every morning, thinking she might have to find a new route if the Gruesome Threesome would be there. That was the name she'd given them in primary school, though she'd never said it aloud. They were the opposite of gruesome, of course, the three prettiest girls in the school, if not the town: Sandra was the daughter of a solicitor, Patricia Dale, the oldest offspring of the local MP, and Debbie Curtis, the only child of a man who owned a construction company. She'd met them at school shortly after her parents moved from Whitby to Middlesbrough. They continued to secondary school and college together, thankfully going their separate ways when Teo went to university.

They'd been a gang then, in their schooldays. Teo was drawn to them not by friendship or shared interests but because they adopted her as someone does with a stray dog.

The Gruesome Three.

And Teo.

And one other.

'What do you know about that body they found on the cliffs?' Debbie Curtis said. 'Is it, you know?'

She observed their expanding eyes and twitching lips, recognising their excitement as morbid curiosity, like when drivers slow down to stare at a traffic accident. However, she knew it wasn't because they wondered if the police had discovered their missing friend after so much time.

'No,' Teo replied. 'It wasn't Annie.'

Annie Hamilton, the only real friend Teo ever had, who'd vanished ten years before on her thirteenth birthday.

'Well, that's good,' Sandra said. 'So, there's still hope.'

Teo stared at her, the most popular girl in school, now a

wannabe Instagram influencer, and wondered if she was being sincere.

'There's always hope, Sandra.'

'Who was it then?' Debbie said.

The sweat dripped off Teo's forehead. 'I can't say.'

They looked at her through disappointed eyes before Sandra spoke.

'When are you coming out with us, Teo? Then we can all have a drink together like the good old days.'

She forced a smile at them. 'I'll text you.'

Teo watched them jog away, knowing it would be a cold day in hell before she socialised with any of them. Instead, she thought of Annie as she headed back to her flat, preparing for another meeting she wasn't looking forward to.

She was at her desk for only a minute when she got the summons from Chief Constable Beckett.

'He refused to leave Redlands?'

Teo peered at the wrinkles in his uniform. 'Detective Inspector Bukowski said he'd think about it, sir.'

He sat behind his desk and rubbed at his chin. 'But he didn't seem upset about his father?'

'No, sir. He was curious about the circumstances, but that was all.'

She was beginning to think he'd forgotten what he'd mentioned yesterday when he brought it up.

'I want you to do me another favour, Teo.' He reached into his pocket, removed a photo, and handed it to her. 'This is Phoebe, my niece. My sister is worried about her.'

She stared at the picture, a teenage girl, perhaps eighteen, with dull blue eyes, bright blonde hair, and perfect skin, looking like she was unaware of how cruel life could be. Teo could only guess what kind of trouble she was in.

'What do you need, sir?'

He sat up and sighed. 'Unfortunately, she's fallen in with the wrong crowd, led by her boyfriend, Darren Carter. You'll find an arm's length of information about him on the computer, mainly drug offences.'

'Do you want me to talk to your niece, sir?'

He shook his head. 'No. Whatever you say to her, she'll only take it as coming from her mother and do the opposite. I want you to speak to Carter to warn him off Phoebe. You can keep the photo.'

She felt the material between her fingers, wondering what to say to Carter to keep him away from the girl. 'I'll do my best, sir.'

She opened the door to leave as he spoke.

'And Teo. Keep this between us. Don't record it anywhere.'

She nodded and left, going to her desk and clicking the computer's icon to access the criminal records database. She retrieved Darren Carter's details in thirty seconds: twenty-eight years old, two short terms in prison, one for drug dealing, the other for assaulting a former girlfriend. She glanced around the building, looking at her colleagues and knowing what they'd think if they knew she was doing this for Beckett without recording it. He could easily deny asking her to speak to Carter if something went wrong.

But she had no choice now.

Teo memorised Carter's address and left the station. The drive was fifteen minutes away, and she spent the time considering what to say to him.

. . .

She drove into the estate, greeted by a barrage of stray dogs yapping and barking like Tory politicians celebrating making cuts to free school meals. Teo passed boarded-up shops and a pub with half a dozen old blokes smoking near the entrance. She parked outside Carter's house, locked the car, and walked up the path. It wasn't much of a garden, with only tufts of dirty grass and weeds spearing out between the junk somebody had dumped there, including a bathtub and a pram. She knocked on the door and waited, listening to the hounds fighting in the street. She pounded on the door, but there was no answer, so she knocked again, and it swung open.

'Hello,' she said.

Silence followed, so she stepped inside, her feet sticking to the carpet. The place stank of soiled nappies and cheap cigarettes as she strode through the corridor, glancing into an empty living room before hearing a male voice in the kitchen.

'I'll have the money tomorrow, I promise.' Teo entered, and he saw her. 'I have to go now.' He ended the call and glared at her. 'Who the fuck are you?'

She showed him her warrant card. 'Darren Carter?'

He shook his head. 'I'll set my lawyer onto you for harassment.'

Teo could have left, gone back, lied to the chief constable, and told him she'd done everything she could to protect his niece. Wasn't the girl old enough to make her own mistakes and learn from them? She'd had to, so why shouldn't others?

Then she looked Carter in the eyes and recognised the predator in him.

'Do you know how old Phoebe is, Darren?'

He picked something from his teeth and flicked it against the wall.

'She's legal age, copper.'

'She's not yet sixteen,' Teo lied. 'Her uncle is worried about her.' Did Carter know who he was? It seemed unlikely Phoebe would have told Carter about the chief constable. No small-time crook would surely want to mess around with a police officer's family. 'This is your only warning. If you have any more contact with her, I'll arrest you.'

He snorted like a pig. 'On what charge?'

Teo peered straight into his dark eyes. 'Grooming a minor. Soliciting a minor.' She grinned at him. 'I'll think of a few more.'

She didn't wait for a reply, leaving him to stew and swear in the house. She stepped outside and ignored the dogs in the garden, glad to be away from the stink. Would it be enough, what she'd told him? And if it wasn't, and Carter didn't tell Phoebe to stay away, then what?

Teo pondered the question as she returned to the car, discovering fresh dog shit all down the front wheels. She grimaced and got in, listening to Roxy Music on the radio as she drove away.

Chapter 8

The Journal I

I've wondered for a while if talking to a professional might help, but something has always stopped me. I don't come from a family of therapy-seekers. My northern parents, from working-class homes, would no sooner have pursued such a frivolous thing than become astronauts. My father came from the school of hard knocks, believing men should embrace their masculinity and cut out anything perceived as weak or, God forbid, feminine. But I have to do it. I can't make any more mistakes at work.

Exercise reduces the mania: running or cycling, maybe swimming if I can bear to be around other people. Yesterday at the local pool, I got into a staring contest with a young child, which I lost. A bloke in the next lane stunk of booze and started harassing the women in the exercise group. So I went underwater and whipped off his trunks. Then I left before he could catch me. I might be banned from there now.

The cycling is hard, at least thirty or forty miles, most of it uphill. But I have to be careful I don't get too agitated with inconsiderate motorists or lose control on the road.

Sometimes, they throw rubbish at me; at other times, drivers or their passengers hurl a barrage of abuse my way. Seeing dead rabbits or squashed hedgehogs reminds me of how fragile my life is on a bike.

Yesterday, I stayed in bed until two o'clock in the afternoon. When I finally moved, I went straight to the sofa and turned on the TV, where I watched six consecutive episodes about UFOs and aliens. I drank three pints of water but ate nothing. Between eight and ten, I scrutinised the same news stories on a continuous loop: the climate was in crisis; the country needed more new homes; child poverty was increasing; schools were crumbling; the government was on holiday while the UK stumbled from one disaster to another. Then I lurched back to bed but couldn't sleep. I got up and went to the computer, spending several hours arguing with idiots online. After that, I removed all my clothes from the wardrobe and drawers, folding them half a dozen times before rearranging them in different places. Then, I reorganised all my books by colour before sorting the CDs and DVDs by release dates.

But it was all just window dressing to distract my mind from one thing: Amy Watson. She'd been missing for over a week, and everybody knew it was unlikely we'd find her alive.

I can't write about work – I need this time to escape it.

I've found the best self-treatment for my moods is in creative pursuits. I tried drawing, even taking a few online classes, but gave up when I couldn't draw matchstick cats and dogs. I played the guitar and had lessons when I was younger, but getting back into it was challenging. Having to focus on the strings hurt my brain. So I settled on writing short stories, spending hours in front of the computer and entering them into competitions. At first, I relied entirely on my imagination, dreaming up characters and situations on other worlds. Then I saw them on the screen and realised they were all unimaginative and dull. After wasting days and weeks doing this, I recognised that the thing to do was write something based on my time as a police officer. So I wrote about all the terrible things people do: torture and murder, rape and sadism, lies and deception, life and death.

My mind was a vortex of creativity, overwhelming me wherever I was. And writing about the depravities of humanity did me no good.

So I stopped.

And the hallucinations returned.

My father sits across the table from me, holding the mug with his name and the image of a cartoon monkey on it, a recent birthday present from someone he works with. I guess I'm fourteen or fifteen in this memory. My mother isn't there, and he explains why.

'The Black Dog plagues your mother,' he tells me. I know he's not talking about an animal. 'Do you know what that is, Erasmus?'

I hear the howling in my head and nod. 'I think so.'

'It's a family illness on her side,' he says. Then he smiles at me. 'But it only affects girls and women, so you'll be all right.'

I didn't tell him this talk was unnecessary. My mother's warning signs had always been there. Her fingers would clench and unclench; her lips shimmer with sweat, and her eyelids flickered rapidly before she started talking to herself. These conversations delved between excitement and despair, telling tales of success and failure. Sometimes, I'd get home from school, and she would have rearranged all the furniture to be opposite where it had been when I'd left in the morning. She also had her "creative episodes" – painting the dining room yellow and filling it with bananas, making statues of the royal family out of mashed potatoes, writing a poem, printing it on a hundred A4 pages, and pinning them on the walls around the house. I smile now at these memories, but not all of her actions were so harmless – once, she went to the local supermarket and moved the bleach bottles next to the lemonade. Only my father's intervention stopped the police from arresting her.

My father – the man who vanished but someone who'd never really been there, anyway.

I'm stuck in my life. I feel a braver, happier, more fulfilled person inside me is trying to get out, but I don't know how to reach him. That uncertainty manifests as anger, confusion, solitude, isolation, mistakes, silence, and violence.

Silence and violence.

I need professional help.

Chapter 9

The Unit

Erasmus was showered, shaved and ready for breakfast: one egg, three rashers of bacon, two sausages and a round of black pudding. Life was good - unless you happened to be a pig. He smiled at that thought, recalling when people called him a pig.

Bodies packed the dining room when he got there, like having a bunch of politicians turn up for a moron convention. The residents swarmed over the buffet, the meat eaters grasping for warm, dead flesh, and the vegans and vegetarians behaving much more sensibly. The Marmite tray remained desolate and unloved until he scooped up two sachets for his toast. He missed his regular treats of marmite crisps and marmite cheese from the outside world.

'How can you eat that stuff, Erasmus?'

He bit through a piece of cheese and smiled at Nurse Sapphire Zagadoo.

'You don't know what you're missing, Sapphy. I'm just waiting for somebody to make marmite gin now.'

She narrowed her eyes at him. 'There's no alcohol allowed in Redlands, Erasmus. You know that.'

He tapped the side of his head. 'But I can taste it in here.'

They laughed together, Sapphy talking to the other residents as he finished his breakfast. Then she spoke to him.

'Are you up for a sojourn, Erasmus?'

He wiped a bit of bacon from his top lip. 'How long has it been since I was last outside?'

'Three weeks,' she said. 'But I'd understand if you'd rather not, considering the news from yesterday.'

He took a deep breath and thought about staring into the sea, remembering all those times visiting the beach as a kid. 'A bit of fresh air will do me good, Sapphy.'

She led him from the building. Dr Ramone nodded at them as they left Redlands, and Erasmus wondered when the good doctor would mention the discovery of James Bukowski's remains.

I wonder how many of them think I killed my father?

It was a short walk into the town, and they were peering down at the pier when Sapphy asked the question Erasmus had heard many times.

'What's it like looking at a murder victim?'

He stared at her and wondered if she really wanted to know the truth or for him to sweeten the information. He'd encountered similar people before, those who used to gorge themselves on TV police shows but now fattened their curiosity with true crime programmes.

He gazed out to sea, relishing the warm breeze blowing across his face as the scent of seawater mingled with the aroma of fish and chips from the pier. Then he returned his gaze to his chaperone.

'It's not over for them, even when they're dead.' The wind nipped at his fingers. 'The body is scrutinised and raked over by dozens of people, studied and analysed, photographed and recorded, prodded and picked at, parts cut away, sliced and diced, examined under microscopes, dropped into chemicals, turned cold and hot, placed into boxes and cupboards, stored away and maybe buried after all that.'

Nurse Sapphire Zagadoo, Sapphy to her family and friends, pulled at the starched collar of her uniform. 'What do you mean, maybe buried?'

'Well, sometimes parts can be used for organ donors. Others might feature in teaching and training sessions at colleges and universities; it all depends on the paperwork.'

Sapphy plopped herself onto a bench, looking across the cliff and into the sea.

'So, some people, or bits of them, could be around for years, being handled by students and academics?'

Erasmus reached into his pocket for the cigars he'd stopped smoking a year ago, happy to find it empty. He pulled out some lint and examined it; the trespasser didn't belong to that coat or any other clothing he owned. Someone had been inside his pocket.

'That could happen, depending on what the person or their families signed before or after the death.' He gazed at the beach. 'But it's all relative, Sapphy.'

'How's that?'

'Well, no matter how we die, even if we're burnt on a funeral pyre, the human body will be reduced to the same atoms we all came from and will, eventually, return to the stars and mingle with the rest of the cosmic dust.'

She pulled a packet of toffees from her coat and offered Erasmus one; he accepted it.

'I'm not sure if I'm happy with that.'

He sucked on the sweet, the sugar rush sending a tingle through his jaw.

'Well, unless you believe in an afterlife or discover the secret of immortality, I'm afraid there's not much you, I, or anyone else can do about it.'

A gull landed next to them, and Sapphy picked out the bag of bread she'd brought. She tore a slice into pieces and dropped it to the ground.

'You know I'm a Catholic, Erasmus. I'll be heading to a better life than this when I pop my clogs.'

He swallowed the toffee and laughed. 'Let's hope that's not for many years to come. Didn't you tell me you intended to live to a least a hundred?'

She emptied the rest of the bread in the grass. 'Absolutely, so only another seventy-four years to go.'

Dark shadows crept across Bukowski's face. 'You're twenty-seven this year?'

She grinned at him. 'With those kinds of deduction powers, I can see why you were a top police detective.'

'I'm still an inspector, Sapphy.'

She narrowed her eyes at him. 'You didn't quit when you joined us at Redlands?'

He'd thought about it at the time, of making it easier for his former colleagues, until he realised that giving himself something to look forward to would motivate him to get better.

'No. I'll need to work when I leave, and there's nothing else I can do but be a copper.'

She sighed. 'I know what you mean. I love being a nurse, but sometimes, I think I should pursue a different career.

'You're still singing in that band?'

'The Hex Pistols? Yeah, that's my group: singer and lead guitarist. I know you don't like to venture out at night, but you should come and see us sometimes.'

Erasmus's time outside Redlands was rare, and stepping out after dark triggered his anxiety.

'You're not worried about joining the 27 Club?'

She spat out her sweet, the last bits of it bouncing off the weeds, scaring the birds away, and shook her head.

'You mean the list of celebs who died at 27? I don't think I'll ever be that famous, but thanks for thinking about me.'

He tried not to think of the dead bodies he'd seen in his career but failed miserably.

'Brian Jones, Jimi Hendrix, Janis Joplin, Jim Morrison, Kurt Cobain, Amy Winehouse, and even Robert Johnson all shuffled off this mortal coil at that age.' He stared at her like a concerned parent. 'I have some knowledge of near-death experiences.'

She slipped her arm into his. 'Let's not talk about that now and focus on the mystery of the stolen phone charger.'

'You mean Dr Ramone's missing device? He must have left it down the side of the sofa again.'

Sapphy pulled him along the street, past the shops, pubs, cafes, and restaurants, ignoring the stares of the locals as they went.

'I think you know one of the patients took it because no phones or chargers are allowed on the wards or in the rooms without permission.'

'You mean like mine that only plays music?'

She nodded. 'Dr Ramone agreed to let you have it as part of your therapy.'

He stopped outside a bookshop, and she had no choice but to stand with him; he'd lost so much weight recently but was still strong enough to anchor her there. Bukowski peered at her reflection in the window, watching her through the glass and ignoring the displays of the new

Margaret Atwood novel. However, he made a mental note to purchase a copy soon.

'I've never understood that rule, Sapphy. Is it because the staff thinks we might electrocute ourselves with it, or maybe twist it around our necks and pretend we're the lead singer from Inxs.' He reached to his throat, looking for the marks from a year ago.

She dragged him away from the shop. 'That's not something we should discuss here, Erasmus. You can bring this up in session later if it's bothering you.'

He grinned at her. 'No, Sapphy, I was only messing with you. But even if I knew who'd pilfered Dr Ramone's charger, you wouldn't expect me to snitch on them, would you?'

She crossed her arms and frowned at him. 'I guess not.'

He scratched at the itch running along his nose. His father had called it a boxer's snout, a fighter who'd lost every fight he'd ever had, but it was a nose which had served him well as an investigator until it hadn't, and his world had turned upside down.

He heard his father's voice in his head, reliving their last conversation five years ago before James Bukowski vanished.

'Your mother's illness is not my fault, Erasmus.'

They were standing in the family home in Middlesbrough, which Erasmus hadn't visited too many times since leaving to join the police.

'I didn't say it was, Dad, but you could at least invest more time in her.'

Dr James Bukowski shook his head at his son. 'You know how much of my time I devote to the hospital. Would you rather I spend it with someone I can't help or those whose lives I can save?'

It was the same old argument he'd given since Erasmus had asked questions as a child about why his father was rarely home. He'd never been able to form the right words in response as a kid, but he did then.

'Maybe if you'd spent more time with Mum, she wouldn't be struggling.'

His father smiled at him. 'She'll be getting all the help she needs now. I've seen to that.'

'Yes, you couldn't wait to get her into the care home.'

James Bukowski stared dismissively at his son. 'Would you prefer it if she stayed here and hurt herself? Did you know I came home from work one day last week to discover she'd unplugged the freezer and had water all over the kitchen floor?'

He hadn't argued with his father, leaving to visit his mother in her new residence, knowing it was for the best to get the care she needed. It was the last time he saw his father alive.

'Did you hear me, Erasmus?'

He shook the past out of his head and stared at Sapphy. 'What?'

'We must return to Redlands for your group therapy session.'

'Sure, Sapphy. Let's see what Dr Ramone has for us today.'

REPUS

Chapter 10

The Crime

Sapphy got Erasmus a coffee to take into his session. The cup warmed his hands as he entered the office, immediately noticing the changes in the room.

'You've redecorated,' he said as he sat on the sofa.

Dr Ramone switched off his computer and came from around the desk, taking the seat opposite Erasmus and placing the notepad on his knee.

'Yes, I thought it was time to remove the certificates and replace them with something more soothing.'

Erasmus glanced from the doctor's perfectly tailored suit and back to the walls.

'Why the old black and white photographs?'

Dr Ramone slipped the pen between the pages of the book.

'My grandparents passed away last year, leaving me a mountain of boxes of their things to go through. I never had the time for it until the other week.' He pointed at the framed photos. 'I thought they'd be better here than just gathering dust in the attic.'

Erasmus put his drink on the table. He got out of the

chair, moving to examine the picture of a man with a humongous beard, inside which was a tiny kitten.

'One of your relatives?' he said.

The doctor laughed. 'I'm unsure. It was with the other photos, but there are no details on the back.'

Erasmus scrutinised the other pictures, recognising the location in some of them.

'Are these Skinningrove?'

Ramone nodded. 'Yes. My grandfather worked in the mine until it closed. After that, they moved to Rotherham, where my grandfather and father worked as miners.'

Erasmus glanced beyond the pictures of the nearby village of Skinningrove, staring at the other images he'd seen many times before, striking miners standing in front of rows of uniformed police officers, some on horseback. He knew the stand-off became confrontational not long after those photos were taken.

'Your father was at Orgreave?'

Ramone opened his notebook and removed the pen. 'Unfortunately, yes.'

Erasmus returned to his seat, sipping on the now cold coffee. 'I'm assuming he was never a fan of the police, then?'

He wrote something in the book that Erasmus couldn't see. 'I was only a child then, but I remember my dad returning home looking like he'd just crawled out of a trench in a war zone. My grandfather wasn't well enough to attend the picket, but Dad always described the Battle of Orgreave as a brutal example of legalised state violence.'

He stared at the doctor, peering into his dark eyes and seeing something different in him for the first time since he'd slipped inside Redlands a year ago.

'Is it difficult for you to have a police officer as a patient?'

Another scribble into the notebook. 'Why would it be?'

Erasmus shrugged. 'I've heard stories from coppers who were there, at Orgreave and other pits, where peaceful protests turned into violent confrontations, telling me things that would dismay the general public.'

'Dismay the general public but not you?'

'I've seen too much pain and death as a copper to let it get to me now.'

Ramone tapped the pen on the paper. 'It's been a year since you joined us. How do you view your progress in that time?'

Erasmus glanced at the photos on the walls. 'Have I made progress?'

'Don't you think so?'

Erasmus considered the question. 'I suppose I have. I visited the town today with Sapphy, which I couldn't have done when I arrived here. Other people don't irritate me as much, and my obsessions have reduced.'

More scribbled notes. 'Where are you at with those? Is the number thirteen still a problem?'

Erasmus shook his head. 'No, that's gone.' He scratched at the dimple in his chin, the one his mother had claimed was left by God after He had blessed her only child. 'Last Friday, I woke, and the need had vanished. Just like that, with no explanation.'

'Did something happen on Thursday that might have influenced that?'

'No. I don't think so.' He tried to remember what had happened that day and if there had been anything different in his routine, but there hadn't been.

'Well, okay. So that's more progress you've made.'

Erasmus resisted the urge to press on his dimple as if it were a buzzer for summoning a god he didn't believe in.

He'd done it so many times as a child his parents often found him with blood running down his fingers.

'Yes, I guess it is.'

Ramone put the notebook and pen down and clasped his hands together.

'And how do you feel about your father?'

Ever since DS Andreescu had visited him with the news, he'd known Dr Ramone would ask that question. He'd tried to prepare an answer but struggled to understand his emotions, which was nothing new.

'You mean about his death?'

'Yes. That and the manner of his demise.'

Demise. Erasmus thought that was a polite way of putting it, as if his father had exited this world peacefully.

'There's nothing I can do about it. I wouldn't be allowed to be part of the investigation even if I left here.'

'Would you like to be part of the investigation?'

Erasmus had pictured little else since learning of his father's fate. 'I can't.'

'You can leave here anytime you want, Erasmus.'

He smiled at him. 'Are you trying to get rid of me, Dr Ramone?'

'You've made much progress in the last few months. Perhaps a longer stint beyond these walls will speed up your development.'

Erasmus's smile vanished. 'Is that your expert medical opinion?'

'Yes, Erasmus, it is, but it's your decision. There is no pressure on you to leave if you want to stay here.'

There was a knock on the door before Erasmus could reply.

Sapphy opened it. 'I'm sorry to interrupt, Dr Ramone, but there's another police officer here to see Erasmus.'

Ramone turned to Erasmus. 'Should I send the officer away?'

Erasmus shook his head and stood. 'No. It's so rare to get visitors I should make the most of it.'

He followed Sapphy out of the room, and she whispered in his ear.

'He's in the lounge, a grim-looking bloke with a scar in the middle of his forehead.'

Erasmus rubbed at his dimple, understanding that his former colleagues hadn't sent a lowly DS to speak to him this time.

'Long time no see, Paul,' he said as he approached the man sitting near the window. 'Have you come to give me a belated birthday present?'

'Your birthday was three months ago,' Paul Brennan said.

Erasmus grinned at him as Sapphy left them together.

'I know, that's why I said it was belated.' He scratched some more at his dimple, realising his brain told him he had to do it thirteen times.

Fuck! So much for progress.

He dug up a memory as a distraction. 'What did I get you for your fortieth birthday, Paul?'

'I can't remember that far back, Erasmus.'

Erasmus reached thirteen and pulled his finger from his face, thankful to see no blood there. 'It was only five years ago.'

He scrutinised his friend: tall, dark-haired, handsome – even with that tiny scar on his forehead – well-educated and wealthy parents. He would have been many women's dream date if he wasn't married.

'Five years is a long time,' Brennan said.

Erasmus slapped his leg. 'I remember now. It was two

tickets for the Green Man music festival. You wanted to see John Grant live.'

'That's right, even though you know I hate camping.'

Erasmus laughed. 'Even more than you hate being around crowds?'

Brennan nodded. 'The older you get, the more things you dislike.' He wore a dark blue suit, pristine white shirt, and a tie dotted with tiny Daleks, highlighting his love of science fiction and Dr Who. For a forty-five-year-old man, he looked in perfect health, his clothes fitting him like a glove and emphasising a physique honed by daily visits to the gym. There was an A4 folder near him on the table, with documents sticking out of it.

'Perhaps you need a break from work, Paul. It's done wonders for me. I highly recommend it.'

Brennan picked up the folder. 'You might be right, but it will have to start later. I'm here on official business.'

There's a surprise.

'So, what can I do for you, Detective Inspector Brennan?'

'It's Detective Chief Inspector now. I was promoted nine months ago.'

Erasmus grinned. 'And it's well deserved.'

DCI Brennan gripped the folder, and Erasmus saw the colour drain from his knuckles.

'It should have been you first, Erasmus. You've been a copper longer than me.'

Erasmus glanced around their surroundings, seeing Sapphy and the other staff dealing with the residents, hearing the numbers in his head and knowing they'd stop at thirteen.

'I don't think I was going to get a promotion while I'm in here, Paul.' He pointed at the folder. 'What's in there?'

Brennan also scrutinised the room. 'Would you like to go somewhere private?'

Erasmus shook his head and sat at the table, looking out the window towards the sea.

'No. We have the perfect view here.'

Brennan sat next to him and said the words Erasmus knew were coming. 'It's about your father.'

Erasmus glanced away from the shimmering blue horizon on the water. 'Are you the SIO for the investigation, Paul?'

Brennan nodded. 'Do you have a problem with that?'

Erasmus knew he was only asking to be polite, that Brennan wouldn't turn down a direct instruction from the top brass.

'So, it's definitely murder?'

Brennan put the folder on the table. 'The post-mortem confirms it. A blow to the back of the head.'

Erasmus remembered the last time he'd seen his father, staring at him as he walked away.

'It couldn't have been an accident, maybe from his fall? It's treacherous along the clifftops and dangerously narrow at some points.'

'Not according to the forensic pathologist, Dr Toon. Her report clearly showed that your father was struck in the back of the skull with a blunt instrument. Of course, after five years, it's impossible to say what it was for definite, but she surmised that considering where the body was found, it was likely a rock.'

'The post-mortem can't have been easy for Bella.'

Brennan shrugged. 'She was the only one on duty. And I think she has some expertise in studying old bones.' He grimaced as he said it. 'Christ, I'm sorry for saying that, Erasmus.'

'Don't worry about it, Paul.' He ran his fingers over the folder. 'What's in here?'

Erasmus expected to see Brennan remove photos of the remains, but they were only sheets with typed text.

'I need to review your report from five years ago of what you remembered from the day your dad disappeared.'

Erasmus peered at the top paper, seeing his words and recalling how he'd sat in the police station giving his statement, thinking his father would turn up after another of his all-night benders. He didn't need to look at the documents.

'I took my mother to Morning Wood care home in Redcar. Then I went to my parents' place in Middlesbrough to speak to my father. That was the last time I saw him, on the afternoon of July 31st, 2018.'

Brennan glanced at the papers. 'And what did you talk about?'

Erasmus resisted the urge to poke at his dimple. 'I wanted to know why he hadn't come with me, to say goodbye to his wife but also tell her he'd see her soon.'

'What did he say?'

Erasmus shrugged. 'Some nonsense about how she wouldn't remember whether he'd been there, and it was better for her in the home, where she'd get the professional help she needed.'

'Did you argue?'

The tone of his voice made Erasmus think there was more to the visit than rechecking his original statement. 'My father never argued with anybody. Instead, he waited until you told him what was wrong and quietly refuted everything you'd said. Irrefutable logic was his weapon, not the violence of words or deeds.'

Brennan read from the second paper. 'You claimed later, twenty-four hours after your father's disappearance, that you assumed your father was sleeping off a hangover somewhere after a marathon drinking session.'

'That's right.'

'Yet, officers at the time spoke to his colleagues at the hospital, and they claimed to be unaware of his alleged heavy drinking.'

Erasmus sighed loud enough to get Sapphy's attention in the far corner.

'Dad was a functional alcoholic for most of his life. He never drank at work or before operating, but afterwards, he would have made Oliver Reed or George Best blush. He needed it to relax, was what he told me, because of the stress of holding someone's life in his hands.'

'He performed organ replacements?'

'You know he did, Paul.'

Brennan replaced the papers in the file. 'I find it difficult to believe your father could perform so many successful surgeries if he drank as much as you said he did.'

Erasmus sighed again. 'He never let it interfere with his work.'

'So, you weren't worried when his colleagues reported him missing because you thought he was sleeping it off somewhere?'

Erasmus gripped his legs to stop them from trembling. 'Yes.'

'Do you know where he might go to sleep off such a hangover?'

Erasmus shrugged. 'You should ask one of his mistresses.'

Brennan arched his eyebrows. 'He was having an affair?'

'He had plenty over the years. He never advertised

them, but he also wasn't shy about hiding what he was doing.'

Brennan removed a pen from his top pocket. 'Do you have any names?'

Erasmus shook his head. 'Nope. I was never interested.'

'What about your mother? Did she know about these alleged affairs?'

'Possibly. They probably added to her instability.'

Brennan scrutinised him for thirty seconds before grabbing the folder and getting up.

'Well, thanks for that, Erasmus.'

'You're not going to ask me to leave here to come and help you with the investigation?'

Brennan popped the pen back into his pocket. 'Are you happy here, Erasmus? Do you feel better now than when you were a detective inspector?'

He didn't need to think about it for long. 'Of course, I'm happier now.'

DCI Brennan smiled at him. 'Then why would I ask you to leave Redlands?'

He turned and walked out of the room, leaving Erasmus counting the steps as he went.

It was thirteen minutes past one in the morning when Erasmus decided to return to the outside world.

Chapter 11

The Interview

The blood seemed to move faster through Erasmus's veins. His heart squatted in his throat, head throbbing, pulsating at his temples and behind his eyes, as he tried to shut out the urge to vomit.

Maybe I've made a mistake.

'You've been outside of Redlands before, Erasmus. Only yesterday, in fact.'

He turned to Dr Ramone, fighting the desire to flex his fingers thirteen times.

'Yes, but I knew I could always return here.'

'You still can. But you have to try if you want to continue with your progress. I think you understand that.'

Erasmus nodded. 'Of course, you're right.'

'You'll be fine, Inspector,' Sapphy said next to him. 'And you know where we are.'

He made his goodbyes and got into the taxi. It was a twenty-minute ride to his house in Redcar, and he spent all of it gripping the car's back seat. The journey whizzed past, mimicking the motion of his brain as Erasmus's thoughts stacked up as if they'd been waiting the last twelve months to spring into the world free from the medication he'd stopped taking. The capsules rattled in his jacket, given to him by Dr Ramone in case he felt he needed them.

'It's your choice,' the doctor had told him.

He reached into his pocket for the pills and found a small piece of paper beside them. Erasmus removed it and recognised Sapphy's exquisite handwriting.

This is my mobile number if you need anything. And don't forget The Hex Pistols are playing at The Crown pub this Saturday night.

He smiled as he replaced the note next to the tablets.

They all have confidence in me, so I should as well.

He didn't hang around outside the house once the taxi dropped him off. He'd have to speak to the neighbours, but it could wait. He opened the door and stepped inside, seeing nothing out of place and not a speck of dust. He made a mental note to call the cleaner to let her know he was home.

Erasmus dumped his bag on the floor and went to the kitchen.

I'll get some food online. A trip to the shops can wait a while.

He retrieved his laptop from the back room and sank into the sofa. Surprisingly, the machine started with no problems. He checked his email first, finding a year's worth of junk and spam, but nothing else. He deleted them all before sending a message to work saying he would return in the morning. Then he waited for the shopping to arrive.

Erasmus was sleeping when the doorbell rang. He crept off the sofa, rubbed the slumber from his face and opened the door. It wasn't who he'd been expecting.

'Detective Inspector Bukowski?'

'Did you forget the food?'

'I'm not a delivery driver, DI Bukowski.' He was tall and dressed in a black suit, tie, and shirt. Erasmus noticed dandruff flecked on his shoulders as he reached into his jacket. Then he showed him his identity card. 'Jack Kane, Human Resources from Cleveland Police. I'm here for your back-to-work interview.'

Erasmus shook his head. 'Beckett doesn't mess around.'

Kane put his ID away. 'The chief constable's hands are tied, DI Bukowski. If you want to return to work ASAP, the procedure says you must complete an official back-to-work interview first. I can come back later if you prefer.

'No, let's get this over with.'

Kane stepped inside. Erasmus closed the door and led him into the living room.

'It's a nice house, DI Bukowski. Perhaps you could give me a quick tour.'

He assumed the HR man wanted to know if there were any severed heads in the fridge or if he'd covered the walls with photos of the royal family with their eyes scratched out.

'Sure. Follow me.' They went upstairs. 'Shouldn't this interview have been done at my place of work?'

They stopped at the top as Kane replied. 'Normally, but Chief Constable Beckett thought you'd be more at ease in your own home.'

There was no more conversation as he showed Kane the three bedrooms and bathroom before taking him back downstairs and into the kitchen and dining room. Then they returned to the living room and sat opposite each other. Kane removed a digital tablet from his bag and switched it on.

'Will you record this?' Erasmus said.

Kane nodded. 'Is that okay?'

Erasmus shrugged. 'Sure, why not?'

'Great. So, how do you feel?'

'Starving. I thought you were my food delivery.'

Kane's grin revealed a small gap in his front teeth. 'Are you well enough to resume your duties?'

'I'm fighting fit, Mr Kane, ready and raring to strike fear into the hearts of Teesside's criminals.'

'Indeed. Are you taking any medication, and if you are, are there any side effects we should know about?'

Erasmus peered beyond the HR man, staring at the capsule of lithium pills sitting on top of the TV.

'I'm drug free. I haven't even touched a drop of alcohol in over a year.' Of course, he didn't mention the six bottles of wine and the case of cider he'd ordered online.

'Excellent.' He gazed into the digital screen and avoided Erasmus's gaze. 'Is this a recurring or ongoing condition?'

Erasmus laughed. 'Only as much as life is a recurring and ongoing condition.'

Kane's smile had vanished. 'Did anything related to work contribute to your absence?'

Erasmus ignored the invisible fingers clawing at his guts.

'I wondered for a while if talking to a professional might help, but something always stopped me. I don't come from a family of therapy-seekers.' He took a deep breath. 'Bipolar disorder may evolve over time, making it difficult to diagnose. Sometimes, it's preceded by other conditions, like extreme insomnia, eating disorders – eating too much or not enough – or panic attacks or anxiety. Some people try to control these conditions using drugs and alcohol, which might further obscure the symptoms. This can prevent a correct diagnosis. And, even for those diagnosed, the interval from onset to diagnosis is commonly ten to twenty years. So, what I have has always been in me and has nothing to do with my job as a police officer.'

Kane's expression was unmoving. 'Okay. Can we implement any changes to make it easier for you to attend work?

Erasmus thought about it. 'Extra biscuits in the kitchen and tell DCI Brennan he needs a different type of aftershave.'

Kane didn't smile. 'Do you have any questions?'

'Sure. Did I pass?'

Kane put the tablet away and stood up. 'I'll contact you later today, DI Bukowski, once I've spoken to Chief Constable Beckett.'

He held out his hand, and Erasmus shook it.

'Great. I look forward to the good news.'

Erasmus showed him out of the house just as the food delivery arrived. He watched Kane enter his car while deciding to have red or white wine with his pizza.

Chapter 12

The Return

A crescendo of noise greeted him as he strode into the station, but it wasn't to welcome him. Instead, he stood in the doorway, watching as a large woman tried to strangle a man half her size while screaming obscenities at him. In his mind, Erasmus switched out the foul language for less offensive words.

'You flaming bunt. I'm going to flip you over for this.'

'You're early, sir.'

He turned to see DS Andreescu next to him.

Erasmus nodded at the commotion as a group of uniformed officers dragged the woman off the man, who stumbled into a desk, knocking a laptop onto the floor as he clutched his throat.

'What's that about?'

'Fraud,' she replied. 'The little bloke is her cousin. She needs a kidney transplant ASAP, but it's a three-year wait on the NHS. She doesn't have enough money to go private, so she tried another route.'

Erasmus flinched as the red-faced woman swung her massive arm and knocked a constable sprawling to the floor.

'So, he said he could get her an illegal donor with a surgeon to perform the transplant?' Andreescu nodded. 'How much did he charge her?'

'Five grand. He spent it all on prostitutes and the horses.'

He whistled. 'No wonder she's upset.'

The woman finally calmed down as the little man sobbed on the floor.

'The chief constable wants to see you, sir,' Andreescu said.

Erasmus sighed. 'Is his office in the same place?'

'Yes, sir.'

He left her as the little man threw up over a uniformed officer, striding down the corridor and noticing nothing had changed in the building during his time away. Erasmus didn't knock on the door, walking straight into the office of Chief Constable Samuel Beckett.

'You're missing all the excitement in reception, Sam.'

Beckett glanced up from his computer, his startling resemblance to George Clooney still something Erasmus found amusing. On the wall behind him was the Queen's Police Medal, awarded for his services to policing. Next to that was a framed card from his former colleagues at the National Crime Agency.

'Every day is different in the force, Erasmus. You know this. Would you like a coffee?'

Erasmus shook his head and sat opposite his superior officer.

'Will you take it easy on me so I can ease back into work?'

Beckett smiled at him. 'Of course not. There's already a suspicious death waiting for you.' He stood and came around to the other side of the desk. 'I'm sorry about your dad.'

Erasmus peered beyond him, glancing at the family photos and the certificates on the walls. Amongst them were several pictures of Beckett shaking hands with prime ministers and home secretaries.

'It was always the likeliest outcome, Sam.'

Beckett crossed his arms and leaned against the desk. 'I know, but discovering he was murdered must be hard on you.'

'Has Bella completed her post-mortem?' He wanted to speak to her about it, but knew Beckett wouldn't want him anywhere near the investigation.

'Dr Toon sent the details to me this morning.'

He tried not to stare at a photo of Beckett with his arm around Boris Johnson.

'Are you going to tell me them, Sam?'

The chief constable sighed. 'Dr Toon has confirmed your father died from a blow to the back of the head, possibly from a stone where the remains were discovered.'

'This was near the circle statue on Saltburn cliffs?'

'It was. Somebody likely killed James and hid the body in the bushes.'

'And nobody found it for five years?'

'My understanding is it's quite remote.'

'Walkers go past that spot all the time. I was there once and a photographer was filming a wedding shoot.'

Beckett crossed his arms. 'So, you have visited there?'

Erasmus glanced at the clock on the wall behind the chief constable and wondered where thirteen was on the face.

'I'd assume half of the able-bodied people in East Cleveland have been up there at some point.'

'When was the last time you were there, Erasmus?'

He laughed. 'I thought DCI Brennan was investigating my father's death?'

'Is that a problem?'

Erasmus shrugged. 'Why would it be? Paul led the misper investigation into the disappearance five years ago, so it makes sense to put him in charge now.'

'He came to see you at Redlands?'

'You know he did, Sam.'

'And what did he tell you?'

'Not a lot.'

Beckett uncrossed his arms. 'Do you feel okay to be here?'

'I passed my back-to-work interview, didn't I?'

The chief constable nodded. 'You did. Which is why I need you leading this suspicious death case.'

There would be no easing him back into work. 'Suspicious how?'

'A train hit a man at Longbeck this morning. DS Andreescu has all the details. I want you to go to the scene and talk to the driver. There's also a witness to speak to.'

'Shouldn't the BTP deal with that?'

Beckett's face darkened. 'The British Transport Police are currently undergoing industrial action.'

Erasmus clutched his stomach and laughed. 'The BTP are on strike? I thought our political overlords had outlawed all strike action in this country?'

'This is no laughing matter, Erasmus. I'm sure the prime minister and home secretary will resolve the situation soon, but for now, I want you and DS Andreescu to investigate this unfortunate incident.'

Erasmus shook his head. 'This would be the same

Tweedledum and Tweedledee who cut 20,000 officers and closed nearly 1,000 police stations?'

Beckett sighed again. 'Thank you for reminding me, DI Bukowski, why you won't be in the station when the home secretary visits us next month.'

Erasmus laughed. 'Damn! And that was the whole reason for me leaving Redlands.'

Beckett went to his chair, and Erasmus knew the meeting was over. He left the office and returned to his desk, ignoring DS Andreescu's gaze and turning to his computer. A dead body on the railway would be an interesting way for him to get his brain back into gear, but there was something he needed to do first.

He accessed the NCA's central database of missing persons and located the report for his father. Unlike children, adults had a legal right to disappear, and he'd been convinced five years ago his father had done just that.

And how wrong had I been?

The first thing police must establish is the level of risk to the missing person. As people rarely go missing without reason, police forces are advised to consider "missing" as an indicator of a problem in someone's life rather than an event in itself. So initially, the police review known hazards and look at other factors related to the person's ethnicity, religious beliefs, gender and sexuality. This then decides the speed and scale of the initial response, where everyone missing is divided into low, medium and high-risk. Because Erasmus had been adamant his father was on a bender celebrating getting rid of his wife, Dr James Bukowski's disappearance was initially seen as low-risk.

Beckett and Brennan might not view me as a suspect in my father's death, but maybe I'm to blame since I was so flippant when he vanished.

He looked through the report, reading what he already knew.

Dr James Charles Bukowski was sixty when he disappeared from Redcar on Wednesday, 11 July 2018. He was last seen leaving his local pub after spending the evening with friends watching the World Cup semi-final between England and Croatia. After Wednesday night, there were no confirmed sightings of Mr Bukowski and no contact with his friends or family. Dr Bukowski's son, Erasmus, claimed his father often disappeared for long periods of drinking sessions. Dr Bukowski's wife, Amelia, could not speak to the officers because of her dementia. She moved into a specialist nursing home the day Dr Bukowski disappeared.

He skimmed through the rest of the details, unsurprised the police concluded his father had voluntarily upped sticks and left. His wife was in a care home, and he was only a few weeks away from taking early retirement from the hospital. So what was there to keep him on Teesside? Certainly not his only son.

Erasmus moved the screen away and pushed all thoughts of his father from his head.

I have to visit my mother.

The last time he'd seen her, the day before entering Redlands, she hadn't recognised him. But perhaps she would now.

He reached into his jacket and touched the bottle of pills. He didn't need them, but they reminded him of what he had to lose if he returned to his old ways. The noise in the station increased as Paul Brennan entered, and his colleagues greeted him with high fives. Erasmus looked at his former friend and wondered if he'd made some progress in the investigation. Teo dropped a folder on his desk before he could get up and ask Brennan.

'Do you want me to drive to Longbeck?'

He smiled at her. 'I thought we might walk there.'

She scowled at him. 'It's five miles away.'

'Aren't you a keen jogger, DS Andreescu?'

Her scowl increased to consume most of her face. 'Who told you that?'

'There are no secrets in a police station, Teo.'

She glanced at his computer screen. 'Are you sure?'

'What's that supposed to mean?'

Teo grabbed the folder. 'Nothing, sir. Do you want to look at the initial reports before we go?'

Erasmus stood. 'I'll read them on the way. But if you're driving, then I choose the music.'

She scowled. 'It better not be old man's rock music.'

He laughed as they left, wondering when being forty turned him into an old man.

Stop
Look
Listen
Beware
of trains

Chapter 13

The Train

Kraftwerk's "Trans Europe Express" drifted out of the radio as Teo drove to the scene. Erasmus flicked through the information the uniformed officers had gathered as the car stopped at a red light.

'The victim is thirty-four-year-old Jack Trent, resident of the Lakes Estate and customs officer at Teesside Freeport.'

'Low taxes and levelling up,' Teo said.

He rested the folder on his legs. 'What?'

The light changed to green, and she drove off. 'That's what the government promised when they converted the port into a low-tax special economic zone.'

Erasmus checked the Freeport website on his phone. 'A secure customs zone where business can be carried out inside a country's land border, but where different customs rules apply. They can reduce administrative burdens and tariff controls, provide relief from duties and import taxes, and ease tax and planning regulations. But, while located geographically within a country, they essentially exist outside its borders for tax purposes. So, what's wrong with that?'

Teo gripped the steering wheel. 'This government is obsessed with cutting taxes. The theory seems to be cutting taxes, which then gives people more money to spend, stimulating producers to create more goods and heigh-ho along comes economic growth. For a start, only those who earn a lot will benefit from tax cuts – the poorest don't pay taxes. And how are producers suddenly going to produce more goods? They'd need extra labour. But hang on, there's a labour shortage. So, they'd offer higher wages and offset them by charging more for the goods. Even without the extra production, they'll be able to charge more for the goods already in production. In both cases, inflation is the result. And what if the extra money from tax cuts is spent on hoarding assets or buying shares? The fundamental problem is that profits are paid out in bonuses and/or given to shareholders rather than invested in industries for the future. None of this helps create a fairer society.'

'You've given this some thought.'

She nodded. 'And they're dredging the seabed to increase the size of the port, which is creating all sorts of environmental problems and killing thousands of crabs.'

He slipped his phone into his pocket. 'I missed a lot while I was in Redlands.'

Teo glanced at him. 'Didn't you have access to the media or the internet?'

'Sure, if you wanted to, but I had to escape the outside world. My brain was on overload, and I needed to reset it.'

She parked on a residential street. 'We'll have to walk from here.'

Erasmus stopped her before she got out of the car. 'If

we're going to be working together, there's something you should know.'

He didn't want to talk about himself, but one of the conditions he'd set himself for leaving Redlands was not keeping any more secrets, especially from those he worked with.

'Okay,' Teo said.

'In the same week my father disappeared, I took my mother to a care home for her dementia. The day after, I was called to a suspicious death in a high-rise flat in Middlesbrough. The woman was in her late seventies with no relatives or close friends. She'd lain dead there for at least two weeks. The front door was unlocked, an upturned table and chair in the living room, and open drawers and cupboards appeared ransacked. The scene convinced my colleagues she'd been killed in a burglary gone wrong, possibly by drug addicts. A witness gave us descriptions of two well-known druggies. We brought them in and grilled them, even though no evidence connected them to the woman's death. Even before we let them go, it was all over the neighbourhood about what they'd allegedly done. But closer inspection, confirmed by the post-mortem, established she died from a fall. It also established what I'd thought at the scene: dementia riddled her brain. I'd pictured her moving through the flat in confusion, knocking over the chair and a small table, pulling things out of the drawers and cupboards, and all because she'd probably been searching for something only she knew about.' He took a deep breath. 'I was the only person at her funeral.' Erasmus glanced at Teo as they stood near the car. 'I'm telling you this because one of those lads we questioned about the old woman's death was murdered not long after in a so-called revenge attack for the woman.' He looked beyond her at the ground and counted the leaves at his feet. 'Never be shy in speaking your mind during an investigation, no matter how ridiculous you might think your theories are.'

Teo nodded. 'Yes, sir.'

He smiled as if invisible hands had lifted a great weight from his shoulders.

'And don't call me sir unless we're before the chief constable. Call me Erasmus. Now show me where the unfortunate Jack Trent died.'

They walked across a field, dodging the dog walkers and striding over a football pitch. He touched one of the goalposts as he went, the feel of it reminding him of his days in the school team.

Teo must have read his mind. 'Redcar Station has a five-a-side team in the county league. It includes men and women.'

'That's new,' he said. 'Are you part of the team?'

'I played once against South Bank Station.'

He grimaced. 'I'm surprised you walked away from that one. There are a few knee crunchers over there.'

She laughed. 'They weren't happy about losing 10-1.'

They reached the end of the field and stepped into the shadows of the trees. Erasmus stared at the Green Lane Footpath Access across the train lines. Beyond the gate was a warning sign to beware of the trains. He opened the gate and moved close to the lines.

'Remind me what our witnesses saw.'

They'd left the folder in the car, but Teo didn't need it to recall the details.

'The driver sounded the horn even though he said the line was clear.' She pointed at the gate they'd come through and then at the one on the opposite side. 'They do it every time they approach a crossing, whether or not anybody is there.'

'Then what happened?'

'According to the driver, it occurred so fast it made no difference when he slammed on the emergency brake.' Teo strode down the line, and he followed, stopping at a gap in the trees. 'Jack Trent came out of here and hit the train full-on.'

Erasmus studied the ground and the tracks, seeing bits of red where the clean-up people missed some blood. He put one foot on the closest track and felt a slight vibration running through it. Then he heard the howl of the horn, so loud it scared the birds from the trees. Teo grabbed his arm and dragged him into the shadows. He was still catching his breath when the train thundered past them. The velocity scooped up leaves and sent them swirling around Teo and Erasmus. He waited for the train to disappear in the distance before wriggling from her grasp and stepping back into the light, trying not to think of the impact the speeding train would have had on Jack Trent's body.

'From the driver's description, that sounds like it was an accident. Or perhaps a suicide.'

'The first officers at the scene agreed until another eyewitness came forward. He was walking his dog on the other side of the level crossing and claims he saw somebody push Trent in front of the train.'

'Where was this witness standing?'

Teo moved across the tracks and stood at the other access gate. 'Here, opposite the incident.'

Erasmus joined her and examined where Trent had died. Then he returned to the gap in the trees where the unfortunate man had allegedly been shoved. There was a clear line of sight between the two positions.

'Did our witness describe whoever pushed Trent onto the tracks?'

She shook her head. 'All he saw were a pair of big arms.'

Erasmus stared at the train tracks, imagining Trent stumbling into the train's path and realising he had less than a second to live.

'Is this your first murder case, Teo?'

She thrust her hands into her jacket pockets. 'We don't know if it's murder.'

'You think it was a prank gone wrong?'

Teo shrugged. 'We only have one person's word that Trent was shoved before the train. The driver didn't see anybody else. And eyewitnesses are notoriously unreliable.'

'That's true.' He peered at the tracks, counting the steps between them to remove the image of blood and body parts covering the area. 'Do we have an address for this second witness?'

She nodded. 'It's in the file in the car. I don't think it's far from here.'

'Okay, then. Let's see if they have any decent biscuits.'

Chapter 14

The Redlands Journal

I haven't shaved or showered in days. The house is full of unwashed plates, pans, cups, glasses, and cutlery. I think I might have had a party at some point, inviting every stranger I met. An unpleasant smell lingers on everything as I drag my fingers through dirt and dust. Piles of broken CDs sit in the corner near a mountain of pages torn from numerous books. The TV is on with the volume muted, so I turn it up. America and China are sabre-rattling, and I wonder if I should join the army because I know I could save the world.

I took guitar lessons as a teenager, dreaming of being the next Keith Richards, Jimi Hendrix, or Mick Ronson. Then, after leaving school, joining the police meant I had little time for hobbies. As a result, I stopped playing the guitar and writing songs that never got beyond my brain or the page. Then, about a decade ago, I re-engaged with the instrument, using that part of my creative brain that had been dormant for too many years. Regular online lessons kept me practising, and I immersed myself in it for hours. Apart from work, it was the only thing I did, transporting me from the grim excesses of the criminal world. During my hypomanic periods, I could connect with music in a way that made me feel more alive.

Hypomania is a milder form of mania with similar but less severe symptoms and causes less impairment. This is affecting me daily and making it difficult to do my job. I can sense my colleagues at the station watching me all the time. I've overheard them talking about me – they think I'm following in my father's footsteps and drinking too much. Some of them think I'm associating with the drug dealers in the town. I could say that all their theories are wrong and it's the hypomania directing my behaviour, but that would be worse. I'd rather they thought I was an addict.

During a hypomanic episode, I have an elevated mood, feel better than usual, and am more productive. I get more work done when I'm in that state. If the chief constable knew how the hypomania had helped me solve more cases, he might want all his officers to be like that. However, it can rarely be maintained indefinitely and is often followed by an escalation to mania or a crash to depression.

My OCD is getting worse. The first thing I do when I wake in the morning is flex my fingers thirteen times. Thirteen was my lucky number as a child, but this is new, something that started when I arrived at Redlands. I brush my teeth thirteen times, scrub between my toes thirteen times, and count to thirteen before leaving my room. I could control the OCD before, ensuring it didn't adversely affect my work, but things have changed now I'm here. I need to know why.

Fears: I've lived all my life fearing nothing, yet now I'm consumed by terror in everything I do. These are the things I'm afraid of – physical contact, fear of losing or forgetting important information when throwing something out, inability to decide whether to keep or to discard things, fear of losing things, fear of rejection, fear of ridicule. Not all of these fears possess me at once, fluctuating daily.

Distractions: at times, I'm distracted by everything, but some things are worse than others: people on their mobile phones near me, a fly crawling up the wall, a badly folded newspaper, pages bent over in a book; people laughing; yellow clothes; the noise of the TV.

I'm speed writing but writing too slowly to keep up with my brain. I feel like my thoughts are running at a hundred miles an hour, but I can only write at half that speed, which is why everything is a mess in this journal.

My senses sometimes overload. Every colour is ten times brighter than it should be. Certain music will make me weep or burst out laughing. My sense of taste and smell is dialled up to eleven, so everything tastes or smells like the best and worst things in the world. My memory has sharpened, becoming crystal clear so I can remember all that's ever happened to me, returning to when I was a baby. This is a problem because some of those memories are of my father's rage or my mother's sadness, and those emotions are transferred to me, making me dangerously angry or deeply depressed. Lights can be so bright they trigger blistering headaches. I don't want anyone to touch me because I'm too sensitive. It seems to worsen in waves, and I never know when they'll come.

My mind is plugged into a generator, electricity surging through me, so I'm desperate to create something, write, paint, sculpt, dance, or sing. And nobody should have to suffer watching me dance or hearing me sing.

I sometimes feel things crawling over me, invisible insects burrowing under my flesh. This is why I have scratch marks over my arms, legs and chest: I've dug my nails into my skin to get the insects out of me.

My anger will flare up for the most trivial things: people eating loudly, somebody whistling near me, hearing people say how much they admire our useless prime minister, seeing Jeremy Clarkson's face, listening to jazz music, getting stuck behind slow drivers on the road; drivers not indicating before they turn. But, in truth, there are too many to mention.

I thought writing this down would help, but it hasn't.

So, I don't know what to do next.

Chapter 15

The Witness

Erasmus stared at the front door.

'Do you know the place?' Teo said.

He nodded. 'It used to be a butcher.'

'You shopped here?'

'Sometimes. The butcher's wife owned the shop, and the building was turned from a house into a butcher with a flat above it. There was a rumour he was taking extended lunch breaks for some afternoon delight down the road. The wife discovered his shenanigans, kicked him out, converted the place back to a residence, and sold it.'

Teo screwed up her face. 'Infidelity is a terrible thing. That's why my parents split up.'

Erasmus looked at her, calculating whether she wanted to discuss her mother's and father's problems. Before he could speak, the front door sprang open, and a mutt came bounding out. The whippet leapt at Teo, who grabbed it in her arms as it stood on two legs and drooled all over her.

She rubbed its head. 'Hello there. So what's your name?'

Erasmus grimaced as the dog got more excited, curious

if she thought the hound would speak to her. Then, a short, stocky, bald bloke appeared from the house.

'She's called Debbie.' He glanced between them. 'I've already given you lot my statement.'

Teo let go of the whippet as it returned to its master. 'How do you know we're police officers?'

The man laughed. 'No offence, love, but Stevie Wonder could spot you as a copper from a mile away.' He scrutinised Erasmus from top to toe. 'Mind you, he looks like the singer from Poxy Music.'

She narrowed her eyebrows. 'Poxy Music?'

Erasmus removed his warrant card from his jacket and showed it to the bloke.

'They're a local pub band covering Roxy Music, Bolan, and Bowie songs, amongst others. I'm Detective Inspector Bukowski, and this is Detective Sergeant Andreescu. Are you Martin Dash?'

Dash flashed yellow teeth as he grinned. 'My mates call me Marty, but you can call me Mr Dash.' He narrowed his eyes at them both. 'Bukowski and Andreescu? You're not British.'

Erasmus replaced the ID in his pocket. 'I was born and bred in this country, Mr Dash, and raised on The Beatles and the Stones, the Pistols and The Clash. I was even an extra in *Atonement* when they shot it in Redcar. I have every episode of *Fawlty Towers*, *Black Adder*, *Rising Damp*, and *Father Ted* on DVD. With a diet of roast beef Sunday dinners, fish and chips, warm beer, and apple pie.'

Dash didn't look convinced. 'Apple pie is American.'

'Apple pie is a longstanding symbol of America, but the dessert didn't come from America, and neither did the apples,' Teo said. 'Apples are native to Asia and have been in America about as long as Europeans. The early colonists of Jamestown brought European apple tree cuttings and seeds with them.'

He peered at her as if she wasn't human. 'You sound like one of those annoying Amazon talking machines.'

'Can we come in, Mr Dash?' Erasmus said.

Dash grabbed the dog by the collar. 'Sure. I may as well talk to you instead of watching daytime TV.'

They followed him inside, and Erasmus held his nose to ward off the smell of unwashed feet mixed with the aroma of a blocked toilet. He glanced at the faded paper on the walls and strode across the sticky carpet.

'Don't eat the biscuits,' he whispered to Teo as they moved into the living room.

'Take a seat,' Martin Dash said.

The sofa looked about as inviting as a sandwich from Jeffrey Dahmer. Teo removed her notebook as a pasty-faced man on the TV expounded the virtues of buying gold coins with a picture of Nigel Farage on them. A Union Flag was hanging over a fake fire.

Neither Erasmus nor Teo sat down.

'Can you tell us what you saw on the level crossing this morning, Mr Dash?'

The dog wagged its tail at his legs. 'You mean about that lad getting thrown in front of the train?'

'Did you see that?' Erasmus said.

Dash held up his hands. 'That's what I told those other coppers. Aren't you paying attention?'

Teo smiled at him. 'We just need to clarify what you witnessed.'

He frowned at them. 'I was on the other side of the tracks cleaning up Debbie's shit when the lad came stumbling out of the trees, two thick arms pushing him forward.

Then the train squashed him like a bug. I felt like taking a shit myself then, I can tell you.'

Erasmus glanced at the whippet. 'You were picking up your dog's poop?'

'Of course. I'm not one of those dirty buggers who leave their dog shit everywhere. Mind you, they're not as bad as those annoying bints on horses. They never clean up their shit.'

'Horse manure doesn't contain diseases harmful to humans, unlike dog excrement,' Erasmus said.

'What do you mean by bints on horses?' Teo asked.

Erasmus intervened before things got heated. 'So, you're claiming you saw somebody push the victim onto the tracks even though the train was coming?'

Dash wiped his nose on his sleeve. 'That's what I keep saying. I'm not blind.'

Teo scribbled into her notebook. 'How could you see what happened on the other side of the tracks if you bent down to clean up the dog mess?'

Dash shook his head. 'Jesus, where do they get you coppers from? I was back up by then and saw somebody shove that poor lad to his death.'

'Could they have been messing around, and it was only an accident?' Erasmus said.

'No. The train horn had blared ten seconds before it got there, and those arms threw the lad into it. So it was no accident.' Dash took a deep breath. 'When you find who did it, I'm going to sue them for the trauma it caused me.' He clutched at his chest. 'I'm suffering from PMT because of it.'

Teo put her notebook away. 'PTSD.'

'Whatever,' Dash said as the dog jumped into his lap.

'Thank you for your help, Mr Dash,' Erasmus said.

'We'll see ourselves out.' Then he pointed at the Union Flag. 'That's upside down.'

He left the room and stepped out of the house. Teo wasn't far behind.

'I need a hot shower and will have to fumigate my clothes after that.'

He agreed. 'Do you believe him?'

She shrugged. 'Why would he lie? He's got nothing to gain.'

Erasmus nodded. 'Did officers knock on doors at the houses on the other side of those trees Trent stumbled out of?'

'I'm unsure. Were you really in *Atonement*?'

Erasmus sighed. 'I was a corpse on the beach, so I didn't get to meet Keira Knightley.'

Teo laughed. 'Well, maybe you can be in a future *Pirates of the Caribbean* movie. You've got that look of a pirate about you.'

He scrutinised his clothes, knowing he needed to buy some new clobber. Then he moved to the car. 'Okay. We need to set up a murder investigation team and question those residents. But first, we have to see a woman about a body.'

Chapter 16

The Post Mortem

Death's perfume irritated Erasmus's nose as they entered the mortuary. He acknowledged those already there: the staff, a uniformed police constable and somebody he hadn't seen in over a year, the forensic pathologist, Dr Bella Toon. Her green eyes sparkled as she smiled at him.

'How nice to see you again, Erasmus.' She glanced at the body parts spread before her. 'Though I don't think there's any doubt about the cause of death.'

He watched the PC grimace as Bella picked up the decapitated head and peered into its lifeless eyes.

'That's Jack Trent?' Erasmus said.

'The one and only.' She pointed at the rest of Trent on the table. 'Your hard-working colleagues have been scrambling around the railway tracks, putting body parts into black plastic bags in the pouring rain.' She put the head down and picked up an evidence bag. 'The contents of his trouser pockets are here – wallet, ID with address, and probably house keys. Remarkably, they survived the impact.'

Teo grabbed the bag.

Erasmus tried not to stare at Trent's dead face. 'Such a terrible way to die.' He glanced at the screen in the corner used for viewing post-mortems from outside the mortuary.

Bella nodded. 'I feel sorry for the poor driver. I once saw a cow explode from being hit by a train, which was gross.'

Erasmus couldn't help but laugh. 'I'd forgotten what a weird life you've had. Was that when you were travelling around Europe alone?'

'It was. I'd just completed my medical studies, and your father told me to travel and enjoy myself.' She looked wistfully at him. 'Swimming with sharks, climbing the pyramids, and naked skydiving. My life has never been the same since. The only excitement I get is playing tennis three times a week at the club.' She laughed. 'Some members were caught having sex in the Jacuzzi.'

A kettle boiled behind them, letting out a high-pitched scream.

'Jesus!' Teo shouted.

'Dr Toon, meet DS Teodora Andreescu,' Erasmus said.

Bella switched the kettle off. 'Would anybody like a cup of tea?' Everybody shook their heads. 'I can't work without a hot drink inside me.' She filled a mug and dropped three sugars into it. 'I'd offer you a sandwich, but somebody ate the last one just before you arrived.' She glanced at her assistant as the PC grimaced. Then she stared at Teo Andreescu? 'You have Romanian ancestry, detective sergeant?'

Teo nodded. 'My great-grandparents went from Transylvania to Whitby.'

Bella grinned. 'The Dracula route – I'm impressed.'

Erasmus didn't feel like laughing, though he could understand why Toon did. She wasn't disrespecting the deceased, only trying to keep a terrible situation as normal as possible.

'The driver slammed on the brakes as soon as Trent stumbled onto the line, but it was too late, dragging him under the wheels before the train could stop,' Teo said.

Dr Bella Toon sipped on her steaming tea. 'He'll have been cut apart like a hot knife through butter. Not much bleeding as the pressure has a way of cauterising the wounds. Death would have been instantaneous, so the heart stopped and didn't pump too much blood out of the various parts. The bones are completely fractured.' She looked straight at Bukowski. 'The cause of death is clear. So why are you here, Erasmus?'

'We have a witness who claims he saw somebody push Trent in front of the train.'

Bella submerged two more sugars into her drink. 'So, it's murder?'

Erasmus nodded. 'It looks like it. Does anything seem suspicious about the victim?'

'You want to know if there are any illegal substances in his system?'

'Is there?' he said.

'I'll have the toxicology results for you later, but for now,' she twisted Trent's head around so they could see the back, 'you might be interested in this.'

Erasmus peered at the bear tattoo on the neck. Teo used her phone to take a photo.

'Anything else?' Erasmus said.

Bella moved body parts to the middle of the table. 'Bruises on the arms and marks on the wrists indicate somebody held him tightly within a few hours of his death.'

Teo took more photos. 'So, someone might have dragged him there and thrown him onto the track?'

'Why wouldn't he fight back?' the PC asked.

Erasmus watched Dr Toon finish her tea. 'That's why we need to know if he was drugged.'

Bella pushed the mug close to the decapitated head. 'Would you like to see what's in his stomach?'

'It's still intact?'

Bella nodded. 'Remarkably so.'

She told an assistant to bring the torso to her. Erasmus noticed the small tattoo of a butterfly in the middle of the chest, imagining a spectral version of it flying into the clouds when the train hit Trent.

'Are you okay?' Teo asked the PC. His grimace increased, but he claimed he was fine.

Dr Toon performed a long incision down the front of the torso and pulled the skin to the side before removing the internal organs.

'Well, this is interesting.'

Erasmus's eyebrows flickered. 'What?'

Bella reached into the stomach and removed something looking like a small version of the face-hugger creatures from the *Alien* movies, dripping in blood and other viscera.

'Christ!' the PC said before he put a hand over his mouth.

Bella laughed. 'Don't worry, constable, it's only a crab.'

Teo took several photos of the crustacean, half the size of Toon's palm. 'How did a crab still in its shell get into the victim's stomach?'

'Someone forced him to swallow it,' Erasmus said.

Bella nodded. 'That seems the likeliest explanation, though he got lucky it didn't choke him.'

Erasmus gazed at the crab. 'Perhaps it did.'

The forensic pathologist placed it next to the decapitated head.

'You think he was dead before somebody pushed him in front of the train?'

Erasmus wasn't sure. 'Is it possible to determine that?'

Bella scrutinised the body parts. 'Luckily, the heart and lungs are still intact, so they should tell me if he was dead before the train hit him.'

'It might be one of those poisoned crabs,' Teo said.

'What?' the PC said.

Teo looked at him. 'In the last year, thousands of dead crabs and lobsters have washed up on the Tees estuary and neighbouring north-east beaches.'

Erasmus peered at the crab. 'I read about that online this morning. Hundreds of dogs reportedly fell ill after walking on the same beaches. The government published a report announcing that the mass death of sea creatures was caused by an "algal bloom" – a rapid increase in the algae population that can release toxins into the water and affect other wildlife.'

Dr Toon shook her head. 'Utter nonsense. No analysis was published, no data, no evidence of any kind. The first dead crabs were washed up in October, and an algal bloom then is highly unlikely around here. Such blooms require high temperatures and clear water, yet the sea was almost certainly too cold then. There was another mass death of crabs and lobsters on the same beaches in February. Again, an algal bloom in October is improbable; one in February is impossible. Then, last month, another mass stranding of crabs and lobsters on the same beaches. Divers reported that the seabed immediately south of the River Tees was a "dead zone." Even the seaweed was dying. And the government still hasn't published evidence for an algal bloom causing the mass deaths.'

'Is this a hobby of yours, Dr Toon?' Teo asked.

'My father was a fisherman,' Bella said. 'And my husband has a small boat he uses to catch crab and lobsters along this coast. Two months ago, he and several others sailed into the mouth of the Tees while setting off flares and fireworks in a protest over the marine deaths, calling for a new investigation. Independent research points to the culprit being a chemical released from sediments in the water caused by dredging the Tees.'

This conversation appeared to have distracted the PC from the body parts nearby.

'Why are they dredging the river?' he said.

Bella poured herself another mug of tea filled with sugar. 'It's needed for the construction of the Freeport. The channel needs deepening for ships to dock at the new South Bank Quay in the Tees estuary. This means excavating historic sediments likely to contain the chemical legacy of Teesside's old industries. That's what's killing the sea life, but the government won't admit it. They have too much invested in the Freeport.'

Teo laughed. 'Freeports are a magnet for money-laundering, tax evasion, corruption, smuggling, counterfeiting, drug trafficking and the distribution of terrorist money.'

'That's all fascinating,' Erasmus said, 'but I don't see how it connects to the possible murder of our victim.'

Bella stared at him. 'If we discover where the crab originated, it might lead to whoever killed him.'

Erasmus shook his head. 'The fishing boats along the Tees coast catch thousands of crabs yearly, poisoned or not. There's no way to trace where that one came from.' He looked at Dr Toon. 'Is there?'

She shrugged. 'I wouldn't think so.'

He took a deep breath and peered at Trent's remains before turning to Teo.

'Wait outside for me. I need to speak to Dr Toon in private.'

It was an instruction for her, the PC and mortuary assistant. They all shuffled out of the room as he stepped closer to Bella.

'I'm sorry about your father,' she said. 'If it weren't for James's support, I wouldn't have completed my training in Manchester.'

'Thank you, Bella. Can you tell me what you discovered at his post-mortem?'

'The report isn't finished.'

He narrowed his eyes. 'Why not?'

She touched his hand. 'There were only bones left, Erasmus.'

He'd expected that. 'DCI Brennan and Chief Inspector Beckett told me you'd determined that a blow to the head murdered my father.'

'That's the likely outcome, but they've slightly jumped the gun from my initial assessment. I haven't completed your father's post-mortem.'

'What's the problem?'

'In temperate conditions, the human body starts decaying quickly. Fluids leak out, and tissue falls apart. Within minutes of death, flies and other insects show up. If there are large scavengers around, they might come for a meal or two. Given some time, the insects will consume all the tissue. Bacteria will do their part. Fungi will get in there, also. All the tissue will be consumed within weeks to months, and only bones will be left if they haven't been scattered and cracked open by scavengers. In five years, pretty much only the bones and a few bits of tissue will remain unless it's a very wet resting spot for the bones. In which case, the bones will deteriorate. It makes it harder to determine the cause of death. But ...'

'But what?'

'There was a break on the back of your father's skull, which could have come from a fall. Or it might have been from a blunt instrument. DCI Brennan told me the remains were discovered under mud and leaves in a remote spot. These might have occurred naturally over time if your father had fallen.'

'Or somebody could have murdered him and covered his body, knowing it was unlikely to be found.'

She nodded. 'That's also possible. I need to do a closer analysis of the bones once I've finished my other work.'

'I understand, Bella. Fresh bodies take priority over five-year-old bones. Do you think he died soon after his disappearance?'

'Yes,' she said.

He thanked her and left the mortuary, finding DS Andreescu talking to the PC.

'You're driving again, Teo. We're going to the victim's house.'

Chapter 17

The Post-Mortem II

It was Teo's first time in the mortuary. The hum of the fluorescent lights gave it the feel of an ambient rave concert she'd attended recently. But there were no aromas of booze and sweat, only the sweet and cloying odour of decomposition. She ignored the smell and noticed a familiar face amongst the staff, PC Frank Croft, who looked green around the gills. Teo guessed it was his first time at a post-mortem as well. Then she saw the mesmerising eyes of Dr Bella Toon, admiring the only female forensic pathologist in the county.

Dr Toon spoke to DI Bukowski as if they were old friends, but Teo focused on what was in front of her – Jack Trent's remains. An image of the train hitting him and what the force did to the body played in her head. Her skin tingled as she heard Toon talk about exploding cows. She picked up the bag containing Trent's possessions and used her gloved fingers to go through them: thirty years of age with an address in the Lakes Estate, Redcar. There was also a membership card to a local snooker club and a recent ticket to a Middlesbrough FC match. She shuddered at the sight.

I was at that game.

She'd been a Boro season ticket holder since transferring to Cleveland Police from Whitby, though she had nobody to go with. Her match day – or night – routine was always the same: walk to the ground from her flat near Albert Park, only stopping for a warm pie and cold cider before heading for the Riverside.

Her grandfather had loved football, telling her plenty of stories of games he went to in Romania, but it wasn't his interest that got her into the game: somebody else did that.

Annie Hamilton.

'You can't support Liverpool or Man United – they're just for glory hunters. And never ever think about following any of the London clubs. Us Teesside girls have to stick with the Boro.' Then she gave Teo her first MFC scarf.

Less than a year later, Annie vanished.

Teo still had that scarf. She'd run her fingers over it so many times in the last ten years it was fraying around the edges, but she would never get rid of it.

She listened to Toon talking about her trips abroad. Teo and Annie had always spoken about travelling the world, spending hours at each other's houses, and dreaming of all the exotic places they'd visit together.

And they never got to do any of that.

A kettle screeched behind her, so she nearly jumped out of her skin.

'Jesus!'

She refused a hot drink, conversing with Dr Toon about her family heritage. The forensic pathologist mentioned Dracula as Teo stared at the bloodless body parts and decapitated head nearby. Then she changed her focus, scrutinising DI Bukowski as he spoke.

I know nothing about him apart from the rumours spread around the station.

Some officers thought Bukowski was involved in his father's murder. That's why he'd entered Redlands last year. There were whispers that guilt affected his mental health and made him behave erratically. But nobody had supplied her with any information when she tried to get details about this supposed erratic behaviour.

And she wasn't one to believe rumours. There had been enough spread about her over the years for her to realise why malicious people might lie about others.

Teo thought about the problems she'd had at university as Dr Toon revealed the bear tattoo on the neck of the deceased. She used her mobile phone to take a photo. Then she took more pictures and wondered if someone may have dragged Trent to the scene against his will, pushing him in front of the train.

PC Croft turned pale when a mortuary assistant brought Trent's torso over. Teo watched Dr Toon perform an incision down the front of the torso and pull the skin to the side before removing the internal organs. Seeing it didn't upset her, though she imagined it was a metaphor for how her life had been taken apart since losing Annie so long ago. And it wasn't only the fact that she was gone; it was made worse by not knowing what had happened to her.

Teo scrutinised Erasmus Bukowski as Dr Toon pulled a crab from Trent's stomach. She recognised something behind Bukowski's eyes – fear of uncertainty about somebody's fate. She'd seen it when he returned to the station, assuming it was because of his father's death. But after spending the day with him, she wasn't so sure. Now, she thought it might be for someone else: Amy Watson.

She continued thinking about the missing girl as the group talked about dead crabs washing up on local beaches. Dr Toon appeared to be an expert on the subject.

'We should go to the beach,' Annie told her in a memory. 'We'll catch some crabs.'

And they had. Annie took the crabs home in a bucket and was surprised when they all died a few days later. They returned to the beach, getting the train from Middlesbrough to Redcar to bury the crabs in their natural environment. It had been Annie's first encounter with death – but not Teo's – and she turned vegan because of it. That had brought the snarky comments out at school, but Teo and Annie had knocked them back together, standing firm whenever they were threatened.

Annie was never out of her thoughts, but being in the mortuary close to the remains of Jack Trent made her memories more painful than usual. She focused on what Dr Toon was saying to push the pain from her mind. Laughter slipped out of her, but she didn't feel happy.

'Freeports are a magnet for money-laundering, tax evasion, corruption, smuggling, counterfeiting, drug trafficking and the distribution of terrorist money.'

Bukowski frowned at Teo before asking her and the PC to wait outside. They left the mortuary and the hospital, Croft heading straight for the smoking shelter.

'Don't tell anybody at the station, but I need this after what I've just seen.'

'At least you didn't throw up,' Teo said.

Croft's fingers shook as he took a drag from the cigarette. 'I swallowed a little bit when she cut the stomach open.'

She nodded. 'I know what you mean.'

'It didn't bother him though, Bukowski, did it? There was no emotion on his face.'

'Detective Inspector Bukowski has been a copper longer than you or me. I guess you get used to these things.'

Croft shook his head. 'I could never get used to that.'

He finished the cigarette as Bukowski came out of the building. He waved the plastic bag containing Trent's possessions at her.

'You're driving again, Teo. We're going to the victim's house.'

Chapter 18

The Town

A plague of adolescents swarmed out of the nearby secondary school, clogging up the pavements and wandering onto the road without a care in the world. Teo watched Erasmus staring at the primary school across the street, guessing what he was about to say.

'That's Amy Watson's school.'

Teo was still in Whitby when the young girl disappeared, but she'd followed the story in the media.

'There was nothing to connect the mother and stepfather to her disappearance?'

He shook his head. 'Amy left school and walked through those shops ahead of us, but didn't go home. She continued on, and there was a sighting of her going into Kirkleatham Woods. That was the last anybody saw her.'

Teo focused on the kids milling in the road. 'What time was this?'

'Five o'clock. Winter was in full swing, so it was already dark.'

She shook her head. 'Why didn't one of the parents collect her?'

He sighed. 'The mother was spaced out on drugs in the kitchen while the stepfather was in the pub. Those were regular occurrences. Amy always made her own way home from school.'

'Where was her biological father?'

'Dead. Amy's mum met Stephen Cook on holiday in Cyprus. He was a soldier in the British army. He died in Afghanistan before Amy was born.'

Teo dodged an errant teenager on a bike and turned left, heading towards the Lakes Estate.

'My mother always picked me up from primary school in Whitby, and for the first two years of secondary.' She gripped the wheel as she drove. 'I hated seeing her outside waiting for me, while all the other kids laughed at me.'

'Overprotective parents are better than ones who don't care,' Erasmus said.

Teo glanced at him, wondering if she should ask about his mother and father. She decided against it and returned to the mystery of the missing young girl.

'There were no leads on where Amy Watson might have been?'

The lines under his eyes grew darker by the second.

'Not by the time I left the force on medical leave, but after this length of time, I expect it will have been scaled back.'

She nodded. 'We don't have the staff to cover everything.' She took a deep breath and drove onto the estate where Jack Trent had lived. Teo parked the car. 'My best friend, Annie Hamilton, disappeared ten years ago. She was thirteen.'

Erasmus undid his seatbelt. 'Over 70,000 children are reported missing each year in the UK. And because many of these kids run away from home and go missing multiple times, there are around 215,000 reported incidents of missing children annually. Children between twelve and seventeen make up more than half of all missing people incidents.'

Teo watched kids stream into the estate, heading for their homes; boys and girls kicking footballs, others riding their bikes, while a few trundled across the pavements on scooters. She looked at Erasmus as they stepped out of the car.

'So, you think because there are so many missing children, it's impossible to find all of them?'

'There's only so much the police can do.' Suspicious residents scrutinised them. 'I remember when Annie disappeared. She was last seen outside the town hall around midnight on a Saturday night, right?'

Teo struggled to breathe. 'We'd been to a party and got separated near the Bottle of Notes. A witness said they saw her getting into a white van, which was the last anybody saw of her. The police were never able to trace the vehicle.'

'How old were you?' Erasmus said.

Her skin prickled. 'You think it was our fault?' She dug a nail into her palm. 'That's what everybody said then, especially the police.'

'That's not what I'm saying, Teo. I'm just trying to guess your age now.'

She didn't believe him. 'I'm twenty-three.'

He peered deep into her eyes. 'Is that why you joined the force, so you could use the resources to find Annie?'

Teo shook her head. 'No, that wasn't it. I wanted to do something for my community, and this is it.'

'So, you've never looked at the police files for Annie's disappearance?'

She answered his question with some of her own. 'Did

you do that when your father vanished? Will you speak to DCI Brennan about your father's murder? Did you ask PC Croft and me to leave the mortuary because you wanted to talk to Dr Toon about your father's post-mortem?'

He was about to reply when a football flew towards them, heading straight for Teo's face before Erasmus caught it like a professional. Then he kicked it back to the teenage girls on the field opposite them.

'Bringing personal issues into your work never ends well, Teo. That's the only advice I'll give you from my twenty years in the force. Now, where's Trent's flat?'

She removed the keys from her pocket and pointed at a house before them.

'There are four flats in there. His is the top one.'

Erasmus reached into his jacket and got a pair of plastic gloves. 'Protect your hands, and let's hope we find something useful inside.'

She did as instructed, avoiding the glare of several locals and walking to the entrance. Teo located the key and opened the door. She nodded at the sign on the lift.

'Out of order.'

'That's okay,' Erasmus said. 'I'm fit enough to walk up four flights. How about you?'

Teo pushed past him. 'I jog every morning and evening, so I think I'll be fine.'

Empty milk cartons and crisp packets littered the stairs, with a lingering smell of stale urine seeping out of the walls. She held her breath and led him to the top, using the key to open the flat. Teo expected him to tell her to wait for him to go in first, the typical masculine thing all her male colleagues did around her. But, instead, he only nodded for her to lead the way.

She stepped inside, slipping the keys into her pocket as

she scanned the surroundings: a small corridor, clean carpet and freshly painted walls. A compact toilet and bathroom lay on the right, and a tiny bedroom to the left. They peered into both before heading into the living room; beyond that was a kitchen.

'Look for anything that might tell us why somebody killed him,' Erasmus said.

Thanks for telling me how to do my job, she didn't say.

Teo examined the kitchen, finding half-empty cupboards, a fridge containing out-of-date milk, six bottles of beer, and a tired-looking piece of cheese.

There's more here than I have at my place.

She glanced into the living room as she left the kitchen, watching Erasmus pulling the cushions off the sofa and sneezing loud enough to shake the curtains.

'Anything?' she said.

He wiped his nose. 'Only dust and a few old coins. You?'

Teo shook her head. 'Nothing in the kitchen. I'll check the bedroom.'

She left him to it and stepped into the bedroom. There was one small cupboard and a chest of drawers, neither of which contained anything worthwhile. Her knees clicked as she looked under the bed, finding crumpled pornographic magazines and empty beer cans. Then she checked the bed, glad to be wearing gloves, between the sheets and mattress. She was ready to re-join her partner when the carpet squeaked under her foot.

Teo stretched down and moved the rug, seeing the opening between the floorboards. Then she bent her legs and pried the board apart.

'All I got was his work address,' Erasmus said behind her. 'What about you?'

She reached into the gap and lifted out a plastic bag full of twenty-pound notes.

'How about this? There must be a few grand here.'

He stared at the money. 'Just over five thousand pounds.'

Teo dropped them into an evidence bag. 'How do you know that?'

He smiled at her. 'I did a quick count.'

She looked at him with new admiration. 'Why do you think he had so much money hidden away?'

He shrugged. 'Like The Beatles, he didn't want to pay the taxman.'

'Should we take this to the station?'

Erasmus showed her his phone. 'No. I've got his work address from the living room. Let's visit that first.'

'And leave the cash in the car?'

'Unless you want to carry it with you.'

Teo stared at the money. She'd never seen so much in one place and remembered what her mother had said earlier. Then she handed it to him.

'As the superior officer, you should keep it.'

He took it from her. 'Okay. Text the chief constable and tell him what we've found and where we're headed. By the time we return to the station, he should have organised a MIT and SIO for this case.'

'I assumed you would be the Senior Investigation Officer for the Murder Investigation Team?'

He shook his head. 'I've been back at work for less than a day, and the investigation needs a more senior officer than me as SIO. Beckett only gave me this job because he thought it would be easy.'

Teo wasn't sure how true that was, but agreed with him. 'Are you going to get a forensics team over here?'

Erasmus glanced around the room. 'I'm not sure if it's worth their time. Though I think there's something unusual about this flat.'

'What?'

'Well, what would you say is missing from here you would have expected to find?'

She thought about what was there and what she'd seen in the other rooms.

'There's no computer or digital devices.'

He nodded. 'Exactly. And there was no mobile with Kent's remains.'

'It could have been destroyed by the train.'

'Possibly, but let's say it wasn't, and there isn't a phone – even a landline – or computer here. So how did he communicate with people, especially his employer?'

It was a good point. 'I guess we should ask them.'

He put the money bag into his jacket, and she followed him from the flat, locking the door behind her. As they went to the car, Teo wondered what some of the estate's residents would do if they knew Erasmus had five grand in his pocket.

Chapter 19

The Freeport

The money bag was squashed against Erasmus's heart as Teo drove them to the Freeport at the Port of Middlesbrough. They paused at the security booth to show their warrant cards and got directions to the offices of the Border Force. She parked in the first available spot. Erasmus stopped her before she exited the car, touching her arm.

'You've read the Annie Hamilton files, haven't you?'

She stared at his hand, and he removed it. 'And?'

'So you know I worked on the investigation into your missing friend?'

'I know you were the only officer who believed she was abducted. All the others thought Annie had run away with an older boyfriend.'

'That was Paul Craven?'

He watched Teo shiver at the sound of his name.

'I hated him. He wormed his way into her life at a party, and she was besotted with him. I tried to warn her about him, but she wouldn't listen and said I was only jealous.'

He recognised the anger in her eyes. 'Jealous?'

143

'Because she had a boyfriend, and I didn't.'

'She was thirteen, and he was nineteen?'

'That's right.' She took a deep breath. 'I've gone over the reports several times. You were the only one who thought Craven might have taken her. The others ...'

Erasmus wished he knew how to ease the pain she carried with her.

'Annie had run away from home before and been in trouble with the police.'

Teo slammed her hand into the steering wheel. 'Those things shouldn't have made any difference to finding her. She had a stupid argument with her parents, got a train to Leeds, and stole food from a shop when she was hungry. That's why the police spoke to her.'

Erasmus stared at her, silently counting the freckles on her cheeks.

'You're right, Teo. We should have been better than that.'

She gazed at him. '*You* were. *You* tried.'

He glanced away from her pain. 'And I failed. Just like with Amy Watson.'

The silence engulfed them.

Then, they exited the car and headed for the Border Force office. They stepped inside, and Erasmus showed the woman at the desk his warrant card.

'We need to speak to Jack Trent's supervisor.'

She smiled at him. 'I'm Jesse Sullivan.' She glanced at her computer screen. 'Jack's off today, but I can answer your questions.'

He gave her the bad news. 'How long had Mr Trent worked here?'

Sullivan put a hand to her chest. 'That's terrible. Poor Jack. What a way to die.' She regained her composure. 'Jack joined Border Force five years ago. I was part of the interview team.'

'What did he do here?' Teo asked.

Sullivan glanced at her computer screen. 'Our work includes checking all passengers and freight arriving in the UK by air and sea, conducting intelligence-led searches for drugs, cash, tobacco, alcohol, firearms, offensive weapons, plus prohibited and counterfeit goods.' Erasmus assumed she'd memorised that straight from the official website. 'We also support the wider department on high-profile issues such as counter-terrorism, organised crime, tracking modern slavery and human trafficking.'

'Do you see many of those things coming through this port?' he asked.

She smiled at him. 'We do our bit.'

He knew she wouldn't give much away, even to two coppers.

'Was Trent good at his job?'

'One of the best,' she replied. 'We had no problems with him.'

'He must have passed several security checks,' Teo said.

Sullivan nodded. 'At the highest level for his position.'

Erasmus noted the admiration in her voice. 'Did he have any close friends here?'

'Not that I'm aware of.'

Teo made notes on her phone. 'What about possessions he might have here? Did he have a uniform for work?'

Sullivan opened a desk drawer and removed a bunch of keys.

'He kept his uniform at home, but I'll show you his locker.'

Erasmus and Teo exchanged looks. They hadn't found a Border Force uniform at Trent's flat.

They followed her down a short corridor and into another room containing a kettle, microwave, a small fridge, and a dozen narrow lockers. She opened the end one.

Erasmus peered at half a jar of coffee, a few dried-up tea bags, two chocolate bars and an envelope. He grabbed it and felt the card inside. He didn't open it.

'One last thing: do you have a contact phone number or email for him?'

Sullivan shook her head. 'As far as I know, he never owned a phone or a computer.'

'Okay,' he said. 'Thank you for your help.' His mobile vibrated, and he checked it to see a text from Beckett. 'We're needed back at the station.'

Sullivan showed them out of the building, returning to the car. Erasmus removed the card from the envelope as Teo spoke.

'What does the chief constable want?'

He peered at the front of the card showing two bulldogs having sex.

'An update.'

He opened it and read the words written inside in a spidery scrawl.

Can't wait to see you again. My new address is on the back. Steve.

He turned the card over and showed the back to Teo.

'It looks like we're going to Loftus,' she said. 'I've never been there.'

'It's the hive of East Cleveland. DCI Brennan and I used to walk there from Redcar, along the beach to Salt-burn, and then up onto the cliffs. Then we'd meander down into Skinningrove and climb the bank into Loftus.'

And stride past the spot where somebody had killed his father.

All that time, I never knew he was only a few feet away from me. I even sat on the bench near the charm bracelet while he rotted in the bushes nearby.

'That's a long walk,' Teo said.

He smiled as the memories returned. 'It's nearly ten miles, all up and down apart from trudging through the sand on the beach.'

'Did you walk back?'

Erasmus laughed. 'We visited local pubs for a few drinks – cider, then on to the gin and tonics – before getting the bus to Redcar.'

'So, you and DCI Brennan are mates?'

His smile vanished with the memories. 'We were.'

He waited for her to ask why they weren't friends anymore, ready to lie to her, but she returned to the subject of Jack Trent.

'Do you think the five grand we found in Trent's flat was smuggled through the port?'

He shrugged. 'It's possible. Maybe it was payment for something he helped smuggle into the country.'

'Or someone,' she said. 'He could have been part of a trafficking gang, and that's why someone murdered him.'

Erasmus looked at the address. 'The Teesside Freeport is huge, covering 4,500 acres over thirteen sites.' *Thirteen.* 'I guess a few things might slip by the authorities occasionally.'

'Especially if somebody working for the authorities is involved.'

'We don't know that.' He replaced the card in the envelope. 'But we'll have to visit the address in Loftus and speak to the person who gave Trent this.'

She looked at her watch. 'Once we've spoken to the chief constable?'

He shook his head. 'No, we'll do it tomorrow. First, let's give Beckett our update.'

Teo drove away, and Erasmus watched the port disappear behind them as only one thing occupied his mind.

How many times had he walked past his father's murdered body?

Chapter 20

The Team

Erasmus signed the five grand into evidence before meeting Chief Inspector Beckett.

'They've set the Murder Room up at the back,' Teo said to him as she sipped coffee.

He didn't ask her where his drink was. 'We can't have the big room?'

Teo shook her head. 'DCI Brennan and his team are in there.'

She didn't need to add it was for the investigation into the murder of Erasmus's father.

'Do you know who Beckett's assigned as the Senior Investigating Officer?'

'No. I guess he's keeping it as a surprise.'

Erasmus didn't care. Not having that responsibility would help him. The lithium pills were in his jacket pocket, but he hadn't thought about them since returning home. Even the trip to the mortuary to see Bella about his father's post-mortem hadn't set the wrong things off in his brain. Not that she told him much. Still, it had gone well as a first day after a year away. All he had to do now was meet the rest of the Murder Investigation Team, update Beckett, and then he could go home.

A few glasses of wine with a takeaway curry while watching one of the movies he'd missed in the past twelve months, and he could mark it down as a successful return to the outside world.

'I better speak to Beckett.'

'He's waiting for us with the others in the Murder Room,' Teo said.

Erasmus was unsure if that was a good thing or not. He thought about it as he followed her down the corridor, only glancing once at DCI Brennan as he spoke to his team. It was a quick look through the window, but enough for him to see the images pinned to the board, photos of his father's remains. The skull and bones stuck like glue to his eyes as he entered the Murder Room, hearing Beckett's dulcet tones pause as the chief constable saw him.

'I thought I might have to send a search party for you, DI Bukowski.' A ripple of laughter went around the room as Erasmus stared at the others, three young-looking, plain-clothes officers he'd never seen before. 'We can't have the SIO turning up late on the first day, can we?'

He glanced behind him to see who Beckett was talking about.

Then he realised the truth. 'Me? You want me as SIO?'

Beckett nodded. 'DCI Brennan may disagree, but you're arguably our best investigator, Erasmus.'

Erasmus wondered about some familiar faces he hadn't seen on returning to the police station. 'Where's Chief Inspector Matlock and Superintendent Lydon?'

Beckett sighed. 'Matlock retired last year, and Lydon is on long-term sick leave. In fact, the number of officers across the Cleveland force currently absent is the highest it's been for years. So, with that, plus the struggle to recruit new staff, I've requested these three lucky people from other forces for your team. This is DC Martin Rankin, DC Ian Kane, and DC Mel Black. I hope you use them wisely.' Erasmus struggled to respond. 'Now, give me a quick update on today's progress. I have to get to my monthly dib-dib meeting.'

Dib-dib was code for the Freemasons.

Teo handed Erasmus an envelope as he went to the Murder Board. He removed the photographs and pinned them up.

'These are from the crime scene, the railway tracks at Green Lane Crossing.' Then he repeated the details of Jack Trent's death, though he assumed everybody in the room, including the newcomers, already knew them. After that, he updated them on his and Teo's visits to the post-mortem, Kent's flat, and the Freeport. He pinned the card from Trent's locker to the board. 'Teo and I will visit this address tomorrow.'

Beckett grinned at him. 'Not too keen on a trip to Loftus after dark?'

The bottle of lithium pills rattled inside his head. 'No point in working your staff to death, Sam.'

Beckett cleared his throat. 'Okay, good work, you two.' He patted Erasmus on the shoulder. 'I'll see you all tomorrow.'

Erasmus smiled at him. 'Don't have a hangover, sir.'

The chief constable left, and Erasmus turned to his team. He recognised how capable Teo was – as long as she didn't let her sadness for Annie Hamilton cloud her judgment – but he knew nothing about the others.

Five officers for a murder investigation. No pressure there, then.

He scrutinised the newbies: Rankin was ginger-haired

and looked like he went to the gym every morning before coming to work. Kane's bald head and piercing blue eyes made him the spit of the actor Jason Statham. Black resembled a character from *Game of Thrones*, with her white hair in a ponytail. Erasmus expected her to reveal a dragon from behind her, but instead, she asked him a question.

'What would you like us to do, sir?'

He didn't need long to think about it. 'First thing tomorrow, DC Rankin, go to the houses near the crime scene and speak to the residents, check if any of them saw or heard anything, particularly in relation to one or more people heading into that field and trees at the train line. DC Kane question Jack Kent's neighbours about him and his behaviour. DC Black, I'd like you to review Kent's bank account details and see if something unusual pops up. Also, contact the phone companies and check if he has a phone number. DC Andreescu and I will visit the address in Loftus and hopefully talk to the Steve who signed the card about Mr Trent.'

The three newcomers nodded as Erasmus spoke to Teo.

'You should go home and get some rest. It'll be another long day tomorrow.'

'Sure. What about you?'

'I'll do the same.'

He walked away, already feeling guilty for lying to her.

Chapter 21

The Pub

Erasmus didn't go straight home from the station, heading to his local pub first. It sold cheap meals, popular with families and the older generation. He avoided those by finding a seat in the corner frequented by the daily drinkers. He didn't like to call them alcoholics because he'd once been in the same position. So, as he glanced at the day's copy of the *Evening Gazette* on his table, he was drinking a sugar-free glass of Coke.

The headline was about how the country's economic recession affected Teesside, highlighting the growth of food banks, with stories of people unable to afford heating or eating. Only when he reached the third page did he see an article on Jack Trent's death, not that it mentioned his name.

Death on the tracks closes the train line between Redcar and Saltburn for hours.

There was a photo and a small paragraph of text with the barest of details. He read it twice, knowing he'd have to give the media more information sooner rather than later. Next, he skimmed through the rest of the newspaper, searching for anything relating to the discovery of his father's remains, but there was nothing. Only when he checked online did he find reports about the bones discovered on Saltburn cliffs, though there was no mention of his father. He understood why Brennan was delaying the inevitable. Releasing a murder victim's name might bring forward new witnesses, but it could also lead to dragging out the cranks and attention seekers, who would claim to be a killer just to get somebody to focus on them. Yet, like with the Trent investigation, Brennan would have to inform the world whose body they'd found soon enough.

Bones. It wasn't a body, only my father's bones.

He pushed the image from his head as his stomach grumbled. Erasmus grabbed the menu and perused the options. The food was generally terrible in those types of pubs, but he couldn't face the prospect of going home and popping something into the microwave.

I have to learn how to cook for myself again.

Before his problems spiralled out of control, he'd loved spending time in the kitchen, flicking through his mother's family recipes, and cooking for himself. Now, he chose from the pub menu and used the app on his phone to order scampi and chips. As he finished ordering, a large shadow loomed over the table.

'Well, as I live and breathe, if it isn't my old mucker Buck Bukowski.'

Erasmus looked up to see a hulking figure looming over him.

'You know I hate anybody calling me that, Rob.'

It was the name the kids at school had given him, and it always got on his nerves. And Rob Destiny knew that. Not that Destiny was his legal name, but the one he'd chosen when he, Erasmus, and two others had briefly formed a band in their teenage years.

Rob slumped into the chair opposite him and dropped a large hardback book onto the table. 'I had to check it was you, Erasmus, to make sure they hadn't replaced you with a doppelgänger.'

Erasmus stared at his Coke and wished there was rum in it. 'Doppelgänger?'

The big man leant in closer but didn't lower his voice. 'Our overlords are replacing important figures in the country with doppelgängers to control everything we do. It's been happening for decades.'

He sighed. Rob's conspiracy theories had been in their infancy when they were both teenagers but had grown exponentially over the years, fuelled by his obsession with the internet.

'I'm hardly an influential figure, Rob.'

The chair groaned as Rob forced his bones into it. 'That's not true, Erasmus. You're the best copper in Teesside by a mile, and when you disappeared last year, I knew they'd done something to you.'

'I didn't disappear. And who are *they*?'

He didn't answer the question. 'I heard rumours you'd vanished behind the walls of Bedlam.'

Erasmus's guts rumbled again. 'I voluntarily entered Redlands.'

Rob narrowed his eyes. 'Is it true what they say happens in there, about the experiments and electroshock therapy used to burn out dangerous ideas?'

'Dangerous ideas?'

'You know what I mean, Erasmus. The things the Deep State don't want the public to understand, like how those with wealth and privilege keep the rest of us oppressed so they can get richer. The capitalist system necessitates unemployment, poverty and violence, uses the law to regulate it and keeps the masses compliant through media and popular culture.'

Erasmus was glad when a young woman brought his food to the table, thinking it might force the other man to leave. He covered his scampi and chips with vinegar and changed the subject.

'I've returned to work, Rob. Being at Redlands helped me.' He tried not to think about the pills in his pocket, having gone nearly a whole day without reaching for them.

Ron stole a chip from the plate. 'I didn't want to tell you this, but I believe *they* also got to your father.'

Erasmus stopped biting into the scampi in mid-crunch. He paused briefly before swallowing it, feeling the bread-crumbs leaving a bad taste in his mouth.

'What?'

'He was chosen for a doppelgänger as well, but some-thing must have gone wrong, and that's why he vanished.'

Against his better judgment, he asked the question. 'Why would the Deep State want to replace my father with a doppelgänger?'

Rob's eyes bulged, and Erasmus realised he was warming to his bizarre story.

'Here's the thing about our secret overlords; it's not only power and privilege they desire, but they also want to live longer than they should.'

Erasmus had a terrible feeling he knew where this was going.

'And they wanted to replace my father because ...?'

Rob fidgeted in his chair. 'I don't think *they* chose him for a doppelgänger, but he was needed because of his skills as a surgeon for illegal organ replacements and blood transfusions: from young, healthy people to those who are old and in poor health. He would have refused, so they snatched him away, and he's never been since.'

Erasmus finished his meal, but something continued to gnaw at his insides.

'When did you formulate this theory, Rob?'

'About the doppelgängers? It's not my theory; it's been online for years, but I adapted it to what I know about Teesside and the strange things that have happened here. Numerous people have spotted UFOs above the cliffs.'

Erasmus glanced at his glass of Coke and knew he'd be opening a bottle of wine when he got home.

'That's fascinating, Rob.' He stood up. 'We'll have to continue this chat another time.'

He watched the big man scoop up the chips left on the plate and exited the pub.

Then he returned to the thought he'd kept at a distance all day.

Who would want to kill my father?

Chapter 22

The Bookshop

Teo didn't go straight home, either. Even though she had hundreds of unread books, she wanted something different to read, so she visited the Waterstones bookshop in Middlesbrough. They were holding a poetry reading event, but it was new fiction she was after.

Her grandfather's love of books had instilled in her the same passion at an early age. She still had prized memories of him reading to her from *The Wizard of Oz*, *Alice in Wonderland*, and *A Wrinkle in Time*. But only when he gave her a copy of *Adventures in Immediate Irreality* by Max Blecher did she discover a connection between her heritage and Romanian literature. She didn't know then that her grandfather was dying, but Blecher's chronicle of his own life and journey towards death touched Teo deeply.

After this, she sought more Romanian novels, buying most of them online: *The Hunger Angel* by Herta Müller, *Musics and Tricks* by Ovidiu Verdeş, and *Little Fingers* by Filip Florian. But on her latest visit to the bookshop, she hoped they could find her a copy of *The Forbidden Forest* by Mircea Eliade.

First, she wanted to browse the other sections. Her love of *Dune*, Ray Bradbury, and film noir also gave her a passion for science fiction, fantasy, thrillers and crime fiction. However, she avoided true crime books and shows because they reminded her of work too much.

There weren't many people in the bookshop, and they lingered around the poetry section for the reading. She grabbed a biscuit from the free food tray and headed deep into the store and away from the poetry aficionados. The only poems Teo had ever liked were *Goblin Market* by Christina Rossetti and a Sylvia Plath collection a former boyfriend had bought her. She dumped him pretty quickly, but kept the book.

The middle part of the shop contained tables of new contemporary fiction, but she avoided those and headed for the science fiction novels. She stared at a massive display of the latest Philip Pullman novel and added it to her To Buy list. Then she picked out a version of *The Day of the Triffids* she hadn't seen before. She'd read it as a teenager and had loved how bleak it was. She sometimes thought about how it might have prepared her to work as a police officer.

'I hate that cover,' somebody behind her said.

She turned to see a tall, thin bloke in a suit and tie. He leered at her before nodding at the book in her hand. Then she glanced at the cover, an illustration of a man with leaves covering his chest and part of his face.

'It's not the end of the world,' she said.

The bloke narrowed his eyes at her. 'I only came over to escape that dreadful poetry reading.' He pulled a copy of *The Hunger Games* from the shelf. 'They should put stuff like this in the children's section.'

It had been a long day, and she was tired, so any thought of diplomacy slithered back into the shadows of her mind. And the hunger pains scratching at her gut made her grumpy.

'I don't know what your problem is, but I'm guessing it's hard to pronounce.'

She heard his knuckles crack as he gripped harder on the novel. 'What?'

'If you need a book on how to chat up the ladies, you're in the wrong place. You'd be better off on one of those incel websites.' She smiled at him. 'Or perhaps that's where you've come from.'

He dropped the book and grinned at her like a vampire. 'You must be one of those modern women who hates all men.'

Teo shook her head. 'No, but I could make an exception for you.'

He laughed at her. 'I earn a thousand pounds a week.' Then he clicked his fingers at her. 'I could buy and sell you like that.'

'Do you get off threatening women?'

His grin turned even more crooked. 'You'd know if I was threatening you, lady.'

He glanced beyond her, and Teo realised nobody was near them in the bookshop. Everybody else was at the poetry reading.

'Is that so?'

He inched towards her, and she smelt the testosterone mixed with cheap aftershave.

'Yeah, that's so. It would be easy to follow you home, wouldn't it? Skanks like you are a dime a dozen around here.'

Teo moved forward, and he flinched. 'I've been called worse by better.'

He regained his composure. 'Don't worry. I've got plenty of time.'

'It's funny watching you try to fit your entire vocabulary into one sentence.'

The darkness in his eyes increased, and she realised she was enjoying herself.

And she understood how wrong that was.

This idiot might leave here and hurt somebody because I upset his fragile ego.

He kicked *The Hunger Games* towards her. 'You should pick that up if you love it so much.'

Teo reached into her pocket, removing her warrant card and showing it to him. He backed off and held up his hands.

'Hey, I was only joking.'

'Unfortunately, stupidity isn't a crime, so you're free to go.'

He staggered past her, knocking a pile of books to the floor. She watched him leave and then picked up half a dozen copies of *Stone Blind: Medusa's Story* by Natalie Haynes. Teo ran her fingers over the beautiful cover and saw herself in the image of the Gorgon's head. She returned the books to the table apart from one. She took that to the counter, paying for it while ordering *The Forbidden Forest*. Then she went and listened to the end of the poetry reading and tried not to think of missing children or dead bodies.

Chapter 23

The Breakfast

By seven a.m. Teo had finished her daily jog and was heading towards the park exit. There had been no encounters with her old school friends, and she hoped the previous meeting was a one-off. She stopped near the war memorial to speak to the homeless man she saw every morning. She reached into her pocket, removed a twenty-pound note and handed it to him.

'What's on the agenda today, Joe?'

He grinned at her through nicotine-stained teeth. 'Oh, you know, Teo, the usual stuff: a visit to the art gallery, then continue with my novel before having tea with the king.'

She wiped the sweat from her forehead. 'I thought you disliked the royal family?'

He nodded. 'Of course I do, the whole lazy, money-grabbing lot of them. That's what I'll tell him over tea and cake.'

The mention of food made her stomach rumble. 'Well, give him my best wishes.'

'What about you, Teo? Got many crimes to solve?'

She shrugged. 'Probably.'

He slipped the cash into his pocket and moved closer to her.

'Be careful on the streets. I've heard there's a new mob of thugs threatening ordinary people.'

She stared at him. 'What gang is this?'

He scratched at the beard covering most of his face. 'The Joker, Goldfinger, Thanos, and Professor Moriarty.'

She shook her head and laughed. 'Okay, Joe. I'll see you at the same time, same place tomorrow.'

Teo left him and jogged back to her flat, needing coffee and a shower, but not in that order.

She was ringing the bell outside Erasmus Bukowski's home at nine o'clock, wondering why one person needed a three-bedroomed detached house with two large gardens, when the door swung open. The space was empty, and she peered into the living room.

'Hello. DI Bukowski, are you there?'

Then, a sudden strange thought struck her.

If somebody killed his father, maybe they're after the son as well: murder a noted surgeon and then a police officer.

But why?

That question possessed her brain as she stepped into the house.

'Erasmus, are you home?'

She closed the door behind her and called for Bukowski again. There was still no answer. She scrutinised the room, noting the flat-screen TV, three-piece sofa, wide coffee table, the Gustav Klimt framed prints on the wall, and the large canvas of Munch's *The Scream* staring at her from the far end. There were two sets of shelves, one full of books and the other containing DVDs. The paperbacks were organised by genre, but she couldn't work out what system he'd used for the movies, but they weren't in alphabetical order. Then she moved closer to them and understood what he'd done – they were grouped by directors: Hitchcock, Kubrick, Tim Burton, Orson Welles, Kurosawa, Fellini, Spike Lee. She ran her fingers across the boxes, stopping – and surprised – by what she found at the end. A section for female directors: Greta Gerwig, Chloé Zhao, Kathryn Bigelow, and others. Teo picked out a copy of *The Decline of Western Civilisation* by Penelope Spheeris and made a mental note to ask if she could burrow it.

That's if I find Bukowski.

Then she smelt the fried food cooking in the kitchen: bacon, sausages and eggs. She put the DVD back, walked through the living room, a dining area, and saw him standing near a frying pan.

'I heard you come in, Teo, but I couldn't stop what I was doing.'

He turned to her, and she smiled at what he was wearing: a pinny with David Bowie's face on it made up like a harlequin.

'I could have been a scary monster,' she said.

He returned her smile. 'Or a super creep.' They laughed together. 'Do you want the full English, DS Andreescu?'

She rubbed her stomach. 'Give me the works. I'm hungrier than I thought I was.'

He piled the food on two plates. 'Toast as well?' She nodded. 'And to drink?'

'Do you have fruit juice?'

'In the fridge. Grab a glass from the cupboard and sort yourself out while I serve the grub.'

Teo opened the fridge, noting the bottles of wine and cans of beer, as she grabbed the carton of orange. She filled a glass and joined him in the dining room. She downed half before speaking.

'This is an unexpected treat. Do you do this for all your work partners?'

Erasmus covered his food in brown sauce. 'Should I have invited the others on the team? I didn't even ask the newbies where they're from.'

Teo bit into her toast. 'Rankin is from Newcastle, though he has no Geordie accent. Kane and Black joined us from Middlesbrough.'

He nodded. 'You spoke to them yesterday?'

'Just a quick word. Five isn't a lot for a MIT, but it's better than nothing.'

Erasmus sipped at his tea. 'Especially with an inexperienced SIO in charge.'

Teo shook her head. 'You've got twenty years of service, sir.'

'He put one hand on the table, and she saw how he tapped a finger on the cloth as if listening to music in his head and beating out the rhythm.

'I told you, don't call me sir unless the chief constable's around.' He peered at the eggs on his plate. 'Maybe I should have invited Beckett to this breakfast.'

'Yes, Erasmus. And no, I don't think you should have invited the chief constable to this gathering. Or the others.' She was unsure what this was all for, but didn't doubt he had some motive. 'There would have been less food for us.'

She tried to lighten the mood, but he wasn't biting.

'My twenty years of experience includes the last year away from the force on health issues.' He dropped two sugars into his tea. 'And since we're working together, I wanted to know how you felt about that.'

She shrugged. 'It's none of my business.'

'But it is, Teo. It might impact you.'

'How so?'

'Do you know why people go into Redlands?'

Of course she did. 'It's a psychiatric unit to help folks with their mental health.'

Erasmus bit through a sausage, and brown sauce dripped onto his chin. He didn't remove it. 'Most people generally say mental health problems, but you didn't. Why?'

'Why should thinking or behaving differently to others be a problem?' she replied.

'Doesn't that depend on the behaviour?'

'Sure, and that means each action should be assessed on several factors and not just thrown together under the umbrella term of mental health problems. For centuries, people, women and girls, in particular, have been classed as crazy or unstable just for behaving outside of what is perceived as conventional or normal standards.'

He nodded. 'You're right, but there's a reason I volunteered to enter Redlands for a year, and you need to know what it is.'

Teo finished her drink. 'That's up to you, Erasmus, but when I spoke to you there, you implied you wouldn't leave anytime soon. Yet here you are.'

'I didn't intend to until DCI Brennan visited me to discuss my father's murder.'

That information surprised her. 'That must have been Chief Constable Beckett's doing.'

He wiped the sauce from his chin. 'Agreed.'

'So why did Beckett send me to give you the news about your father when DCI Brennan was going there, anyway?'

'It's a curious one, isn't it? Why do you think he did it?'

She remembered the personal favour Beckett had asked of her after she'd visited Redlands. 'He was testing me?'

'Sam does nothing without a motive. But what was he testing you for?'

Teo didn't know. 'I'll ask him next time I see him.'

Erasmus dunked a piece of toast in his egg and broke the yoke, so it bled yellow onto his plate.

'What did he tell you when he sent you to Redlands?'

'Not a lot. There's a DI in a psychiatric unit, and I need you to give him some bad news.'

'No mention of why I was there?'

'No.'

'And you'd heard no rumours about me at the station.'

Teo lied to him. 'To be honest, Erasmus, I transferred to Redcar after you left, and nobody spoke about you. Not around me, anyway.'

He cleaned his plate with the bread and laughed as he ate.

'How quickly they forgot me.' He stared straight into her eyes. 'I have bipolar disorder. Do you know what that is?'

She nodded. 'One of the girls in my year at university was bipolar. However, it didn't prevent her from living her life and getting a First Class degree in English.'

'Good for her. But what if I told you that my behaviour deteriorated to where I couldn't function properly in the twelve months before I took my leave? I was unable to do my job properly.'

'Are you better now?'

'I am.'

'Do you take any medication I should know about?'

He removed the pills from his pocket. 'I have these, but there hasn't been a need to use them yet.'

Teo picked it up and read the label. 'Lithium?'

'It's a mood stabiliser if I get very high or very low. It can also help reduce aggressive or self-harming behaviour.'

'Are you prone to aggressive or self-harming behaviour?'

'In the past.'

She didn't push him on it. 'Are there any side effects?'

Erasmus sighed. 'The most common are feeling or being sick, diarrhoea, a dry mouth and a metallic taste in the mouth. But, since I'm not taking the pills, I'm okay.'

'Should you be taking them?'

'Only if I need my mood stabilising.'

She finally understood why he was telling her this.

'You think the further we get into the Trent murder investigation, it might affect your moods so you'll have to take the medication?'

Erasmus nodded. 'It's possible, so I thought you should know.'

'What about the others on the team?'

He contemplated her question for thirty seconds. 'We'll see how it goes. You're the one I'll be working with the most. That's if you're okay with what I've just said.'

Teo didn't hesitate. 'Let's check out this address in Loftus.'

Erasmus got up. 'I won't even ask you to wash up. Now let me leave Mr Bowie behind and get my jacket.'

She grabbed the last piece of toast from the table and watched him replace the pills in his pocket, knowing there was more he wanted to tell her about his reasons for leaving the force.

But it would have to wait.

They had a murderer to find.

Chapter 24

The Village

Erasmus studied Teo as she drove to Loftus, wondering if what he'd told her over breakfast was the correct thing to do.

Of course it was. She saw me at Redlands and had a right to know why I was there since we're working together.

But he still wasn't sure how Beckett and the others at the station were taking his return to the force.

'You can park at the library. The house we want is near there.'

She took his directions and parked on a single yellow line. The sun warmed his face as they got out of the car. Erasmus looked at the GPS on his phone and pointed down the road.

'It's over there.'

He put the mobile away and removed the photocopy of the message from the card they found in Trent's work locker. They reached the house, and he knocked on the door, waiting for 'Steve' to open up.

But nobody appeared.

He tapped again as Teo peered into the window. 'The curtains are closed.'

It was a narrow terraced property amongst a dozen others. She'd checked the property online, discovering a local housing association owned it. Before Erasmus could knock again, a woman stepped out of the house next door.

'There's been nobody there for a week.'

He guessed she spent most of her time peering between the curtains.

'Do you know who lives here?' he asked.

She lit a cigarette and shrugged. 'Some gangly bloke with a twitchy eye.'

Teo wrote the description in her notebook. 'How long has he lived here?'

The woman blew smoke at them. 'About a month.'

Erasmus took out his phone and showed her the photo of Jack Trent he'd copied from the Border Force files.

'Do you recognise him?'

The neighbour scrunched up her eyes and peered at the screen.

'Maybe. He might have been here once or twice. Not for a while, though.'

He thanked her, and they returned to the car.

'I'll chase up the name of the occupier and a set of keys from the housing association,' Teo said.

'Okay,' he replied. 'I need you to drop me off in Skinningrove village first. It's only a few minutes from here.'

She scrutinised his face. 'Is this to do with the case?'

He shook his head. 'It's personal business.'

'How will you get back?'

'I'll walk along the cliffs to Redcar. I've done it many times before, though usually in the opposite direction.'

Teo gripped the steering wheel but didn't start the engine. 'I should come with you.'

He put his seatbelt on and avoided her gaze. 'Why?'

Erasmus heard her breathing increase. 'After what you told me this morning, we should stick together as much as possible.'

'You're not responsible for me, Teo. You hardly know me.'

'That's not the point.'

He turned to look at her. 'You think I might be going up there to jump off the cliffs, don't you?'

She shook her head. 'No. Absolutely not.'

'I'm not suicidal, Teo.'

'I never thought you were, Erasmus, but I know why you're doing this.'

'And why's that?'

She gazed at him. 'You want to see where your father's remains were discovered.'

'So, what if I do?'

She let out a long breath. 'Not that I want to brag, but I'm a good copper, and two sets of eyes on a crime scene are better than one.'

Erasmus smiled at her. 'You're right on both counts.' Then he pointed at the windscreen. 'Let's go.'

The wind had increased when they got out of the car, whipping Teo's hair across her face as they stared at the jetty. She pushed it back and appreciated the view.

'I never knew it was so beautiful down here.'

'It's a hidden gem,' he said. 'There's nothing much in the village apart from houses, holiday rentals, and the Ironstone

Museum.' He pointed at the jetty. 'People still fish from here, but it's not what it used to be.' Erasmus twisted his head to look up at the cliffs. 'We need to be up there.' He glanced at her feet. 'It's a good job you're wearing sensible shoes and not high heels.'

Teo frowned at him. 'I never wear high heels, but I've got better footwear for climbing in the boot.' She went to the car and changed her shoes. 'These are my joggers.'

'Great. You'll be able to run up the hill.'

'Ha, ha. Don't we have to go across the beach first?'

He nodded. 'We might as well take the scenic route.' They walked past the jetty and down to the sand. 'This is Cattersty Sands.'

They avoided the dog walkers and stared into the shimmering blue water. Erasmus inhaled the aroma of the ocean and listened to the gulls swooning above him. He'd forgotten how much he loved being that close to nature. He could see the sea from Redlands, but it wasn't the same. The experience reinvigorated his whole being, so he thrust his hand into his pocket and removed the lithium pills.

It would be so easy to throw these into the water right now.

'Are you okay, Erasmus?'

He returned the medicine to his jacket. 'I'm just preparing for the climb.'

Cattersty Sands was a long, golden expanse of clean sand, with a strip where the water crept up to the foot of the dunes and the steep cliffs overlooking the beach. It wasn't like other coastal strips, with no commercial outlets spoiling the experience: no food stalls, toilets, games, arcades, donkeys or doughnuts.

He trudged across the sand, leading her through the sandbanks and to the narrow steps built into the cliff. Erasmus glanced up, observing the birds scrutinising his first faltering step. Liquid iron filled his legs, forcing his knees to ache and his ankles to throb. One strong gust of wind would have carried him to his death, but he continued moving up, never stopping, even though his lungs called for rest.

It took a minute to reach the top, and Erasmus was out of breath, resting on a board displaying information about the location. Teo caught up to him.

'Are you okay?'

He wiped the sweat from his forehead. 'I'd forgotten how steep that climb was.'

She glanced at his hand, seeing his fingers flex and unflex. She read aloud the information on the display.

'Cattersty Viewpoint on the Cleveland Way.'

'The Cleveland Way is over a hundred miles long, but we're only walking a small part of it.'

She grinned at him. 'That's a shame.'

'Yes, DS Andreescu, there's no need to brag about how fit you are compared to me.'

Teo shook her head. 'So how far away are we from ...?'

'The spot where they found my father's remains?'

She nodded. 'We don't have to go if you've changed your mind.'

Erasmus gazed across the cliffs and into the vast expanse of the ocean. 'If you're tired, you can wait here for me.'

She placed a hand on his shoulder and pushed him forward. 'Lead on Inspector Bukowski.'

He returned her grin, dragged air into his chest, and strode along the cliff to Saltburn. On one side, they had the clear blue sea, while on the other were fields of green with the occasional sheep grazing in the distance. He didn't engage in conversation, focusing on the ground and what he knew lay ahead. The path was rarely flat, dipping up and down as they passed a few other walkers and the odd dog.

After ten minutes, Erasmus stopped and pointed at the derelict buildings nearby.

'We need to be over there.'

'Did DCI Brennan tell you where the crime scene is?'

'No. He won't disclose anything, and if I access the details on the computer, I guess Beckett would come down on me like a tonne of bricks.' He turned to her. 'I suppose both of them are right – it's too personal for me to be involved.'

She narrowed her eyes. 'Sure, but they could keep you updated on their progress. If there is any.'

'Maybe. But what would happen if they told me they had a lead on a suspect? How do you think I'd react to that?'

'I don't know. How would you?'

He shrugged. 'I'm unsure. That's the problem.'

'So why do you want to see where your father's remains were discovered?'

'I just do.'

He continued walking, with the path wide enough for Teo to be at his side.

'If you don't know the crime scene location, where are we going? The forensic team will have removed everything by now.'

Erasmus smiled at her. 'Not everything. There are always little bits of yellow plastic left behind. Look.' He pointed at the bushes leading up to the derelict buildings. 'Can you see them?'

Teo nodded. 'Yes.'

He picked up his speed, nearly jogging through the grass until he reached two large brick walls covered in graffiti. Next to that was a railway track, and just beyond was a stone structure resembling a small church.

'My father's remains must have been found around here.'

'What are these buildings?' Teo asked. 'And where does that track go?'

Erasmus looked at the tracks. 'Those run to Boulby potash mine. The graffitied walls are the foundation of an engine house used for haulage. The building opposite is the fanhouse that ventilated the Huntcliff ironstone mine.'

She noticed several large bushes surrounding the buildings. 'You could hide a body under these easily enough, even for five years. That's until somebody walking their mutt stumbled upon them.'

'What else do you see around here?' Erasmus said.

She scrutinised the whole area. 'Lots of wide open countryside.'

'Indeed, so plenty of space to walk a dog. But because of the sheep sometimes in these fields, dogs should always be on a lead, not that every owner does that. Yet, with all this space surrounding us, why would somebody walk their dog into these buildings and close to a train line?'

Teo shrugged. 'Who knows, but a dog walker found the remains.'

Erasmus touched the wall near him, avoiding the paint and feeling the cold stone on his flesh. 'What you mean is that the person who discovered my father's body claimed they were walking a dog.'

She peered at the fanhouse. 'What else would they be doing here? Graffiti?'

'That's possible, but I was thinking something a bit more intimate. You have some secret you prefer to keep hidden from the police or anyone else, so you invent the story about the dog.'

She thought about it for a second. 'You think they might have been having sex?'

Erasmus nodded. 'I do. And probably not with their recognised partner. It was an illicit encounter, and then at least one person stumbled upon my father's bones.'

'We should tell DCI Brennan about this.'

He shook his head. 'No. Paul's clever enough to work that out himself. Let's talk to this eyewitness first.'

'I thought you wouldn't get involved in the investigation?'

Erasmus smiled at her. 'I keep changing my mind. And anyway, I'd only have a quick word with the person who discovered the remains.'

He waited for her to argue with him, but she didn't. 'Was your father a walker or a rambler?'

'Neither. He had no great love for the countryside.'

'So, what would he have been doing all the way out here?'

'Think about it,' he said. 'Not walking a dog, that's for sure.'

He saw the realisation dawn on her. 'You believe he came out here to have sex?'

Erasmus nodded. 'As long as I remember, my father had a string of extramarital affairs. Towards the end, he didn't even bother hiding them from my mother or me.'

Teo stared at the derelict buildings. 'Okay, but why here? There are plenty of hotels in the area.'

He shrugged. 'Who knows? Perhaps the sense of danger added to the excitement. But maybe the woman wanted to come here.'

'Would it definitely have been a woman?'

The question threw Erasmus. 'You think my father might have been gay?'

She held up her hands. 'Possibly? Some men keep those feelings hidden all their lives, and then, as they get older, they act upon them.'

'Are you speaking from experience, Teo?'

'All I'm saying is if we're running with the theory your father was out here for an illicit assignation, we can't just assume it was with a woman.'

'Understood,' he said. 'But you think him coming here for sex is the likeliest explanation?'

Teo pursed her lips. 'I never knew the man. I bow down to your experience.'

Erasmus walked back the way they'd come.

'Therein lies the problem, Teo. Because I never knew him either.'

Chapter 25

The Gig

Erasmus walked into Redcar town centre. He left home later than expected because it had taken him so long to choose the right clothes. He'd never been one to put much stock in the latest fashions, and since leaving Redlands, had only worn suits and shirts outside the house.

So it had taken ages for him to find something comfortable in a pair of faded jeans bought ten years ago, smart shoes, a new t-shirt somebody had stuck through his door while he was out, and a light coat. He assumed the shirt had come from Sapphy since it said 'Never Mind the Ovaries, Here's The Hex Pistols' on the front.

Erasmus checked his reflection in the window as he strode into the pub. The band was due on stage soon, but the place was only half-full. He went to the bar and bought two bottles of Mexican lager. Turning around, he saw Teo sitting at a table with three other young women in the corner.

She beamed at him, and he guessed she'd already had a few drinks.

'Calm down, ladies. This isn't Harry Styles but Redcar's most eligible bachelor, Erasmus Bukowski.'

He sat with them. 'Who's Harry Styles?'

The four young women gazed at him as if he'd just stepped off the UFO from the end of *Close Encounters of the Third Kind*.

Then they burst out laughing, and he realised he was probably the oldest person in the bar.

Teo slapped him on the arm. 'Nice shirt, Erasmus. You should get these three to sign it for you later.'

He drank half of one of his bottles. 'You're The Hex Pistols?'

The redhead with the dayglow eyes nodded at him. 'I'm Alma, the drummer.' She pointed at the dark-haired Louise Brooks lookalike next to her. 'That's Lulu on bass guitar, and the blonde beauty at her side is our lead guitarist, Rozi.' Then she waved her hand in the air. 'Sapphy is around here somewhere.'

Erasmus raised his bottle to them. 'Nice to meet you all. I'm looking forward to the gig.'

Lulu leaned into him. 'You definitely have his eyes, but the rest of your face is different from his – you're much more handsome.'

He laughed to hide his nervousness. 'Whose eyes? Gary Gilmour?'

The three members of The Hex Pistols collapsed in laughter, but Teo only stared at him. Alma wrapped her arm around his shoulder.

'You'll do for us, Erasmus, if you know your punk history.'

Teo continued to glare at him. 'Wasn't Gary Gilmour executed for murder in the US?'

Alma nodded so hard he thought her crucifix earrings might fall from her head.

'We won't get bored tonight, girls, not with our new friends and their expertise in punk music and American crime.'

Erasmus felt the heat coming from her body and sensed his cheeks turning red, so he tried to deflect his thoughts in another direction.

'Whose eyes do I have, Lulu?'

Her teeth sparkled when she smiled at him. 'Your dad's, of course. You're better looking, but I hope you can dance as good as he did.'

The fiery sensation inside Erasmus turned into a volcano when it reached his chest. He struggled to breathe as he wriggled free of Alma's grasp.

'You met my father?'

'We were a different group then, just me, Alma, and Sapphy in a band called Smog Attack, more pop than punk.'

He downed the rest of the first bottle of lager. The place was filling up, smelling of alcopops and cheap perfume.

'When and where was this?'

Lulu squeezed her eyes. 'About five years ago. It was a charity event at the hospital. I'm not sure if everybody liked our music, but they were pretty pleased by what we wore for the night.'

'What was that?' Teo asked.

Lulu giggled. 'We went as naughty nurses - tight uniforms, short skirts, low-cut tops, black stockings, and enough leather to turn a fetishist's wet dream into reality.' She gazed at Erasmus. 'Your dad was certainly impressed, especially with Sapphy.'

'Are you telling poor Erasmus tales about me?' Sapphy said as she joined them. She dragged Lulu from him. 'Come on; we're due on stage.' She winked at him. 'Nice shirt, Inspector.'

The Hex Pistols stumbled away from the table, climbed on the stage, and grabbed their instruments as Erasmus sat there catching flies.

Teo poured herself a glass of Prosecco from the bottle chilling in a bucket of ice.

'She's your nurse from Redlands?'

'One of them,' he said.

And I thought I knew her, but she'd kept it secret about meeting my father five years ago.

The noise exploded from the stage, clashing guitars and drums loud enough to shake the dust from the ceiling. Erasmus watched the band, all four dressed in tight leather trousers and the same shirt he wore. Sapphy sang about the death of the working class, the collapse of the environment, and women's rights. He listened in a daze during their forty-minute set, wondering if this was how his father had felt five years ago when witnessing something similar.

Teo returned from the bar with more drinks, plunking two bottles of Mexican lager before him. 'Why do people put a slice of lime in the drink?'

He pushed the thin piece of fruit into the bottle and took a swig. The mix of alcohol and citrus set his taste buds tingling.

'Some say the metal caps used to seal the bottles are notorious for leaving rust marks on the rim, so the lime acts as a rust-remover and steriliser. A similar principle applies to the claim that citrus works as a disinfectant, which makes sense considering the drinking water in Mexico is known for its harmful effects.'

She scrunched her face so it looked like an invisible

hand was pushing fingers into her cheeks. 'Perhaps you shouldn't be sipping that.'

He shook his head. 'The lime is part of my five a day.'

Teo laughed and downed more fizzy bubbles. 'I'm glad you asked me out tonight.' She nodded at the band. 'They're great.'

'Yes, they are,' he said.

The Hex Pistols finished to a rousing roar for more. Sapphy stood with her hands on her hips and addressed the audience.

'Okay, this is for my old friend Erasmus and my new mate Teo.'

They then performed a raucous rendition of Blondie's "One Way or Another."

Teo nudged him in the side. 'She's far too young for you, Inspector.'

He scowled at her. 'I know that.'

Erasmus gazed at Sapphy not because he was attracted to her, though he understood she was attractive, but because he wanted to know why she'd kept the secret of knowing his father from him.

The band finished for a second time and jumped from the stage, fending off unwanted attention from drunk blokes but talking to the girls and women interested in their merchandise, which, as far as he could tell, comprised t-shirts and CDs. He got up from the table and walked over to the stand.

'How much do I owe you for the shirt, Sapphy?'

She wagged a finger at him, her purple nail varnish shimmering in the disco lights, bathing them in a glittering illumination.

'Don't be daft, Erasmus. I'm just glad you came and brought Teo with you.' She pulled away from the others and moved closer to him. 'Though I think she's far too young for you.'

He laughed with her. 'That's funny because she said the same thing about you.'

Sapphy put her arm in his. 'Didn't you tell her I'm gay?'

He shook his head. 'She's a detective; she'll work it out, eventually.' He glanced across at his colleague before whispering into Sapphy's ear. 'I need to talk to you outside.'

She pulled at her sweat-stained shirt. 'No problem. I have to cool down, anyway.'

He let go of her as they pushed through the crowd and stepped into the night. The air cooled his face while she waved a hand in front of her. A group of smokers puffed out a stink around them, so they moved towards the bus stop. Across the road, two old men shouted at each other.

'That's just like me in the morning howling at the mirror,' Erasmus said.

Sapphy smiled at him. 'Did you enjoy the gig?'

He nodded. 'You were great. I'll buy some CDs when we go back inside. I'm sure Teo will as well.'

'Fantastic,' she said. 'That might help pay the bills.'

He realised he didn't know where she lived or much about her, apart from her work and being in the band.

'Don't Redlands give you a decent wage?'

She put one hand on her chest and sighed. 'It's not enough to look after two young kids and an alcoholic wife.'

Guilt swept through him. While she'd taken care of him in the unit, Erasmus had never asked Sapphy about her life outside Redlands. He'd told himself it was because he didn't want to pry into her personal life, but he realised now he was being selfish.

'I'm sorry, Sapphy. I didn't know.'

She narrowed her eyes, and he thought she was about to burst into tears.

What would I do then? I'm not very good at comforting people.

Instead, she smiled and laughed at him. 'I'm only winding you up, Inspector. The pay isn't great, barely above the minimum wage, but it's enough for my bills with a bit left over to enjoy myself. Now, what did you want to talk about?'

His throbbing heart returned to normal. 'Why didn't you tell me you knew my father?'

Cigarette smoke drifted between them. 'Your dad? I only met him once at a charity night at the hospital. I didn't know him.'

He scrutinised her face and assumed she was telling the truth while keeping something from him. He was about to quiz her when Teo exploded out of the pub.

'You two better not be snogging out here.'

Erasmus and Sapphy laughed together, though her laughter was more nervous than his.

What is she hiding from me?

The rest of The Hex Pistols followed her out.

'The manager has locked our equipment and merch in the back room so we can carry on boozing, lads and lasses,' Lulu said.

Teo burped loudly. 'Excellent. So where to next?'

'We've got work in the morning,' Erasmus said.

She squinted at him. 'It's Sunday tomorrow, Bukowski.'

It was, and he hadn't realised. He thrust a hand into his coat pocket to ensure the pills were still there. He was about to tell them he was going home when Alma grabbed his arm and dragged him towards her.

'Do you want to miss out on a drunken night with four beautiful young women?'

He gazed into her eyes and recognised he didn't. 'Okay, but the first round is on me.'

Alma punched him in the shoulder. 'Triple gin and tonics all around, then.'

Erasmus laughed and let her drag him away, glancing at Sapphy as she spoke to Teo.

Maybe after a few more drinks, she'll tell me what she's keeping secret about my father.

Chapter 26

The Hangover

He woke with a banging headache and no further insight about what Sapphy was hiding. As well as the hangover, his guilt had grown overnight - remorse for not visiting his mother since leaving Redlands.

I can't keep putting it off.

Erasmus stumbled into the shower and stood under the hot water for five minutes, trying to remember the final few hours of the night.

We ended up in the Blue Lounge at two in the morning, but I can't recall much after that.

He'd tried to broach the subject of his father with Sapphy, but something always got in the way, like Lulu dragging him onto the dance floor when the DJ played Iggy Pop. Or bumping into some bloke he'd put away a few years back glaring at him between the obscenities. Or Teo quizzing him about his love life.

'Who was your last girlfriend?'

The lager had slipped down his throat as he considered her answer.

'How do you know I'm not gay?'

That didn't dissuade her. 'Okay, who was your last boyfriend?'

'I'm still a virgin,' he replied.

He assumed she would take it as a joke. But instead, she told the others, who then spread the news to every woman in the bar. That was the last thing he remembered before getting into the taxi.

I don't even know if Teo got home okay. It's a long way between Redcar and Middlesbrough.

Erasmus climbed out of the shower, dripping water everywhere, searching for his phone. He found it on the floor and texted her.

Did you get home okay?

He dropped the mobile on the bed and grabbed a towel, drying his head first. By the time he'd done his whole body, she'd replied.

I stayed at Sapphy's. We're having breakfast now. How's your hangover?

The room spun, so he sat.

Bad.

You should come here. Sapphy has a perfect hangover cure.

I can't. I have to visit my mother in the care home. I'll see you at work tomorrow.

Okay. Last night was great. We should do it again soon.

Erasmus didn't reply, pulling on trousers and a top. On the back of a chair was his Hex Pistols t-shirt. He left it there and stumbled downstairs.

Last night was great. What I remember of it.

He went into the kitchen and put the kettle on. Coffee would help to clear his head and remove the lethargy in his bones. There was one thing he hadn't forgotten: that Sapphy was keeping something from him about his father.

He left that thought to linger as he prepared to see his mother for the first time in over a year.

And he wondered if she'd still remember him.

He changed his plans as soon as he got into the car, his skull aching so much he couldn't face seeing his mother until his head cleared.

Putting it off again.

Instead, he visited the hospital to talk to his father's colleagues who were still working there.

He went to the oncology department, heading for the office he'd visited several times before his father's disappearance. He saw the sign for Dr Gavin Marsh and knocked on the door. It was a long shot for a Sunday, but Marsh had always been a workaholic, so Erasmus kept his fingers crossed.

And he didn't have to wait long.

'Erasmus, so good to see you again.'

Dr Marsh thrust his hand towards him, and he shook it. Then, the doctor showed him into the room.

'You should take a day off occasionally, Gavin.'

Marsh grinned at him through perfect white teeth. 'Disease and illness never rest, Erasmus, so neither can I.'

It might have sounded arrogant from somebody else, but he knew Marsh was as kind-hearted as anybody he'd ever met.

'Is this because Rose wants you out of the house?'

Marsh shook his head. 'My wife works harder than me. And now I'm on the hospital board as the chief medical officer and virtually living in this building.'

'Congratulations, Gavin. I know you've wanted that position for a while. When did it happen?'

Marsh's smile disappeared. 'You don't know?'

Erasmus's head still throbbed, and his mouth felt like a dirty carpet. He sat without an invitation. 'No. Why would I?'

Marsh grabbed a pen and rubbed his fingers against it. 'Your dad announced his retirement as a surgeon and accepted the position as the chief medical officer at the hospital.' He took a deep breath. 'When he disappeared, the board offered it to me.'

Erasmus's throbbing brain went into overdrive. 'So, if he hadn't vanished, you wouldn't have got the job?'

'No.' He dropped the pen on the table. 'Your father and I were friends. I wouldn't kill him over a job.'

Silence lingered between them for a minute.

'Who said he was murdered, Gavin?'

Marsh swung his computer screen around, and Erasmus saw what was on it.

'The police released the information this morning. Didn't you know?'

Of course he didn't.

Thanks for telling me, Paul.

'Was there anybody who might have wanted to kill him?'

Marsh shrugged. 'All I know is he was supposedly involved in a complicated love affair.'

'Affair?'

'Yes. You know what your father was like, Erasmus. We had to warn the nurses about him.'

'Why didn't you tell me or the police about this when he disappeared?'

Marsh grabbed the pen again. 'It was only hospital gossip. He would never have been invited onto the board if it had been true.'

'Do you know the name of the woman he was allegedly involved with?'

Marsh shook his head. 'As I said, it was only gossip, and I never pay attention to these things.'

'But it might have been somebody working in the hospital?'

The chief medical officer relaxed his grip on the pen and held out his hands.

'It's possible, I suppose.'

Erasmus stared at him for a minute before getting out of the chair. Inside his head, a dozen volcanoes exploded as he promised never to touch a drop of alcohol again. Then he left without saying goodbye. He spoke to a few other staff, but they were no help. There was only one person left to talk to.

It was time to see his mother.

Chapter 27

The Visit

Erasmus parked outside the care home and sat in the car. Jim Morrison wanted somebody to light his fire on the radio as Erasmus peered at the front door. His headache had just about vanished, and he felt ready to face the world: to meet his mother again. Five years ago, he'd collected her from the family home, paying little attention to his father's absence.

He was never there for her or me, anyway.

'Are we going out for afternoon tea?' she said to him.

It was two p.m., and he was worried she hadn't eaten all day.

'Are you hungry, Mum?'

She shook her head. 'James bought me fish and chips earlier.'

He thought nothing of her words then, being too busy getting her to the new home, but they struck a chord in his brain as he waited outside the care home.

Had she seen him the night he disappeared? Did he visit her without me knowing? If so, she might have been the last person to see him alive.

Erasmus gripped the steering wheel. After dropping her off that day, he barely saw her over the following years. Work had kept him busy – so he told himself – and his condition had grown so bad he couldn't think of anybody but himself. Then the pandemic struck, and seeing anyone was nearly impossible, especially those deemed vulnerable. He still thought it a miracle she survived that period, considering how much the government had fucked up its duty to protect those at most risk from the virus.

He controlled his breathing and got out of the car, stepping back when he saw who was exiting the building: DCI Brennan with a young dark-haired woman.

'Are you looking for a bed for the night, Paul?'

DCI Brennan didn't smile. 'Detective Inspector Erasmus Bukowski meet Detective Sergeant Cassie Froome. And vice versa.'

Her grey eyes cut right through him. 'I've heard so much about you, DI Bukowski.'

Froome's gaze irritated the hairs on his neck. 'Nothing good, I expect.'

She shook her head. 'Paul says you're the best copper he's ever worked with.'

Erasmus ignored the platitudes and faced his former friend. 'What are you doing here, Paul?'

Brennan inched closer to him. 'DS Froome and I visited your mother.'

The drummers that had disappeared from Erasmus's skull returned with a vengeance, banging on his brain like a concert celebrating the Apocalypse.

'You've interviewed her?'

His former friend nodded. 'You know I had to, Erasmus.'

'Did you tell her you found his body?'

'We did, but I don't think she understood what we meant.'

'You told me it was murder, but Bella said she hasn't confirmed what killed my father.'

Brennan shrugged. 'Toon says he fell and hit his head, or somebody attacked him, and then he fell. She can't confirm it from the bones, but it's one or the other.'

Erasmus dug his nails into his palm. 'Either way, somebody hid his body in the bushes.'

Brennan nodded. 'Indeed, which is why we're treating it as murder.' He stared at his colleague. 'There's no need to stress about it. We don't want you having a relapse, do we?'

Erasmus pushed past him, digging his fingers into the DCI's chest. He explained at the reception that he'd phoned ahead for an appointment, and a woman showed him into the building.

'Amelia will be pleased today, having so many visitors.'

He glanced around his surroundings, seeing several rooms: a dining area, lounge, TV room, a large space where an instructor took a group of residents through armchair exercises, and a spot where most people appeared to be napping. The clientele was older; otherwise, it reminded him of Redlands.

'Does my mother get many visitors?' he said as the woman took him into a lift, opening the doors with her key card.

She shook her head as they stepped inside and went up.

'I was here when Amelia joined us, and I think you're her first visitor since then.' She peered at Erasmus. 'You were the one who brought her here, weren't you?'

He nodded as the lift juddered to a halt, seeing the accusation in her eyes.

'I was away, so I couldn't visit.'

She smiled. 'Never mind. I'm sure she'll be happy to see you now.'

They stepped into a corridor. Vividly painted flowers covered the walls, and everywhere smelt of lavender. Erasmus heard a song he recognised coming from a room at the end.

'How has my mother been?'

She stopped walking and turned to him. 'She's fine. This is the best place for her, don't you worry.'

They reached the open door, seeing Amelia Bukowski sitting in a chair and reading a book on Hollywood scandals.

'I've brought you another visitor, Amelia.' She pointed at Erasmus as if his mother couldn't see beyond five feet. 'Do you know who it is?'

He watched her grip the book, noticing how she'd lost weight and that her hair was now completely grey.

'He's like an older James Dean,' she said. 'Before that accident ruined his face and a few more wrinkles.'

The woman from reception smiled at him. 'There's always staff on this floor. Just let one of them know when you want to leave, and they'll bring you back down.'

He watched her go, not wanting to enter the room and get closer to his mother. The music continued, and he wondered why she was listening to "Sympathy for the Devil." It finished, and The Smiths' "How Soon is Now?" replaced it out of the portable speaker on the desk.

'I only discovered modern music when I came here. Your father hated anything that wasn't Mozart or Beethoven.'

Erasmus stared at her, floored that she remembered who he was and how alert she appeared. He moved closer, struggling to find the right words, finally settling on the only thing he could think of.

'Where did you get the music?'

She closed the book and rested it on her knee. 'One of the lovely women here does me a mixtape. They keep all the swearing songs away from me, but they're the ones I want to hear.' Her smile lifted his heart, observing the sparkle in her eyes that he hadn't seen in over thirty years. 'Perhaps you could bring me some Sex Pistols, Sleaford Mods, Billy Nomates and Public Enemy, Erasmus?'

He pulled a chair over and sat beside her, touching her arm.

'How are you, Mother?'

"Mysterons" by Portishead drifted around the room.

'Oh, you know, I have good and bad days.' She put her hand on his. 'And when there are people I don't want to talk to, I pretend it's a bad day and just stare at the wall and ignore all the questions. That's what I did with your friend before you arrived.'

Her wrinkles reminded him of Martian canals from a comic he'd read years ago.

'DCI Brennan?'

She tapped his fingers. 'He's been promoted? I remember the first time you brought him to the house. Your father hated that, having other people in his home.' She lowered her eyebrows. 'I thought you would be the one to give me the news about him, Erasmus.'

He took a deep breath. 'That's why I'm here, Mother, but Paul beat me to it.'

She shook her head. 'Well, I forgive you, my son. It can't be easy doing your job. Are you in the same place?'

'Do you mean for work or home?' He couldn't believe how lucid she was.

'Both,' she said. 'And I suppose you aren't married.'

Erasmus laughed. 'Same police force, the same house in

Redcar and, yes, still single.' He shrugged. 'No sensible woman would have me.'

She removed her hand from his, and he felt a sense of unfathomable loss.

'I guess you're not your father's son, after all.'

The music changed to Marianne Faithfull singing "As Tears Go By," and he wondered why the playlist was only playing thirty seconds of each song.

'What does that mean?'

'You know what it means, Erasmus. Your father was never the most faithful of husbands. You must have noticed.'

The meeting was getting stranger by the second.

'I noticed. I thought you didn't know.'

She held up her hands and laughed. 'Oh, come on.' She tapped the side of her head. 'I may have had problems with my memory, but I wasn't blind.'

He digested her words, taking time to collect his thoughts. 'Then why didn't you leave him?'

'Well,' she said. 'I couldn't while you were still a child. And it would have been hypocritical of me to criticise your father for something I'd done.'

The volume increased, the rhythm matching the thumping of his heart, as "Down For Fun" by Liz Lawrence burst out of the speaker.

A single word crawled over his lips. 'What?'

The sparkle vanished from her face, and she retook his hand.

'I've meant to tell you this for years, Erasmus, but things always got in the way. I cheated on your father, not just to get back at him, but to give me some excitement.' She gazed deep into his eyes. 'Do you remember your Uncle Donald?'

His lungs shrunk, and he struggled to breathe, clasping his chest to stave off a heart attack. 'Dad's brother?'

She released him. 'Yes.' His mother peered beyond him, staring at the empty walls as if she could see something he couldn't. 'He was the opposite of your father: charming, witty and attentive. I should have married him, but I chose the wrong Bukowski.'

Realisation dawned on Erasmus. 'Wait. You had a fling with him before and after your wedding?'

His mother grinned at him as Donna Summer sang about feeling love.

'Well, I wouldn't call it a fling. It was much more than that.' Her lips trembled as she spoke. 'For you and me.'

He jumped out of the chair, legs threatening to give way as he stumbled into the wardrobe behind him. The music kept changing, all jumbling into one like a frenzied remix of his life.

'You mean Uncle Don might be ...?'

She glanced at the book on her knee. 'I told your father we could do a DNA test, but he said it wouldn't make any difference. He was right, of course.'

Erasmus could only stare at his mother. He'd gone there to break the news to her, expecting to find a woman who could barely remember her name.

And he'd got this.

She opened the book and flicked through the pages. 'Are you upset about your father?'

'Are you?'

'I lost him a long time ago, Erasmus. We both did.'

He didn't disagree with her. 'Are you well enough to leave here, Mother?'

'Poor Fatty Arbuckle,' she said as she put the book down. 'I like it here, Erasmus, so there's no need for me to go anywhere else. But at least you escaped from Redlands.'

A thousand tiny people attacked his brain with hammers inside his head.

'You knew about that?'

'Oh, we get all sorts of gossip here. You should hear what I know about your chief constable.' She got out of the chair and went to him. 'Will you visit me regularly now?'

The tear in her eye matched his own. He lifted his hand and ran it through her hair.

'Of course, Mother, of course.'

He stood with her for an age, as Marvin Gaye wanted to know what was going on.

Chapter 28

The Investigation

Erasmus had a sleepless night, with a thousand thoughts spinning through his head. His father might not be his dad after all. His mother was lucid and apparently healthy. Sapphy had met his father five years ago and was keeping something from him about that meeting, and Dr Gavin Marsh at the hospital had a good reason for wanting his father dead.

These thoughts consumed his brain, but none made any difference: he wasn't on that investigation. He had to find out who pushed Jack Trent in front of a speeding train.

The Murder Room was busy when Erasmus arrived at work. Teo had a glint in her eye, and he wondered if there was something else he'd forgotten about their night out.

'We've got some updates for you, boss,' she said.

He sat at his desk and stifled a yawn. 'Go on.'

DS Rankin stepped forward. 'I spoke to all the residents who live near the Green Lane Tracks.' He flicked open his notebook. 'Most were away at the time of the death or didn't see or hear anything. All apart from one.'

Erasmus's mind flickered into life. 'And?'

'A retired seventy-year-old man was walking his dog in the field that leads to the crossing. He claims two men stumbled across it, with the larger of them virtually dragging the other with him. I showed him a photo of Trent, and the witness confirmed it was him he saw that morning.' An audible sigh of relief went around the room. 'He also said Trent looked drowsy or barely conscious.'

Erasmus decided there was no point in formality with his new team.

'Good work, Martin.' He turned to Teo. 'Anything new from Bella?'

She nodded. 'Yes. In the tox screening, Dr Toon discovered small amounts of ketamine in his system. Enough to have kept him placid while somebody dragged him to the tracks.'

'Might the drug have come from the crab someone forced him to eat?' DS Rankin said.

Erasmus felt the cobwebs vanishing from his brain. 'It would be a strange way to do it, but I guess it's possible. Maybe Trent loved seafood.' He looked at DS Black. 'Anything useful in his financial details?'

She shook her head. 'I'm afraid not, sir. The only incomings were his salary from Border Force. The outgoings were normal bills and the occasional online purchase.'

'What was he buying?' Erasmus said.

DS Black glanced at her notes. 'Books, computer gadgets, CDs.'

The brief surge of euphoria from Rankin's update seeped out of him.

'Okay. DS Kane: how useful were Trent's neighbours?'

Kane rubbed at his bald head, and Erasmus waited for a genie to appear.

'Most of them wouldn't talk to me, but I got something from a woman who works behind the bar in the local boozer.' He paused, and then the genie appeared. 'She said Trent was barred from the pub last week for fighting with a neighbour, Billy Robinson.'

Erasmus felt all the air leave his lungs.

'Where do I know that name?' Teo said.

Erasmus's lips trembled. 'Billy Robinson is Amy Watson's stepfather.' He addressed DS Kane. 'Did the woman say what the fight was about?'

'She didn't know.'

He put a hand on the desk to steady himself, remembering what had happened the last time he got involved in Amy Watson's disappearance. Then he looked at the photos and documents pinned to the boards.

'I need a coffee.' He got out of the chair before they offered to get him one. 'Talk amongst yourselves.'

He went down the corridor and into the kitchen, seeing DCI Brennan and DS Froome whispering to each other near the microwave. They stopped and turned when they realised he was there.

'How's the Trent case going?' Brennan said.

Erasmus used the coffee maker and poured himself a drink.

'Can I have a word, Paul?' He didn't look at Froome. 'In private.'

The DCI nodded to his DS and she left the kitchen.

'I'm sorry about the thing with your mother, Erasmus, but we had to talk to her.'

Erasmus warmed his hands on the cup. 'Did she tell you anything useful?'

Brennan shook his head. 'She was in a daze most of the time.'

Should I tell him what she told me?

'Where are you at in the case, Paul?'

'You know I can't speak about it to you, Erasmus.'

Erasmus sipped on his coffee. 'I'm not asking for specific details. I'd just like to know if you've made any progress.'

DCI Brennan smiled at him. 'You'll know in due course. Beckett doesn't want you getting distracted from the Trent investigation. You haven't been out of Redlands long, and nobody wants to see you going back there.'

The drink singed his top lip. 'You believe I'm that unstable?'

Brennan shrugged. 'Amy Watson's case was bad for you, Erasmus. It wasn't good for all of us. You need to think about your health.'

Erasmus laughed. 'I'm always thinking about my health, Paul.'

And Amy Watson. I'm always thinking about her. And now we have a link between her and Jack Trent.

'Who's running the Watson case now?' Erasmus asked.

'Nobody,' Brennan replied. 'It's on the back burner until we get more staff or clear the current caseload.'

That was good news for Erasmus. Now, he didn't have to tell anybody outside his team about the link between her stepfather and Trent. However, he should have informed Beckett.

He moved towards the door. 'Make sure you keep me in the loop, Paul.'

Erasmus left the kitchen and returned to the others, finding them sitting around their computers. 'Martin and Ian – return to the pub on the Lakes Estate and quiz the locals about this fight between Trent and Robinson. Mel, please check online for any mention of the two men together. Teo and I will visit Amy Watson's mother, Jane and the stepfather.'

Teo stood next to him. 'How do you want to do this?'

'Simple,' Erasmus said. 'We scare the living shit out of him.'

Chapter 29

The Family

Teo parked opposite the Watson's house.

'Did you interview both of them after Amy disappeared?'

Erasmus stared at his reflection in the mirror, watching the bags grow under his eyes by the second.

'Multiple times, but they had perfect alibis. The mother, Jane, was home with her sister while the stepfather, Billy Robinson, was in the pub. Several eyewitnesses vouched for him.'

'Were there any suspects?'

He shook his head. 'We checked every person on the sex offenders' list within fifty miles of this estate. Amy walked into the woods a mile from here and never came out again.'

'I want you to show me the sight after we finish with Robinson.'

'Sure,' Erasmus said. 'A fresh set of eyes is always helpful.'

They got out of the car, and she knocked on the door,

Jane Watson answered. Her eyes bulged, and she put a hand to her face.

'Oh no, no, no ....'

Teo touched her arm. 'We haven't come about Amy, Ms Watson.' She glanced beyond her and into the house. 'We need to speak to Billy. Is he here?'

Jane Watson regained her composure. 'Billy? Yeah, he's watching the box.'

Erasmus smiled at her and stepped into the house, not waiting for an invitation. He knew the layout by heart, turning left and into the living room. Robinson sat slumped on the sofa, cigarette in one hand and a beer in the other, watching the racing on the TV.

'What do you coppers want now?'

Erasmus thought it interesting that Robinson, unlike Jane, hadn't assumed they were there to bring bad news about Amy. Teo and Jane followed him into the room as Erasmus turned off the TV.

'Hey!' Robinson said. 'This is my house.'

Jane Watson stepped across and snatched the fag from his hand. 'No, Billy, it's mine.'

'Do you know Jack Trent?' Teo asked him.

Robinson's skin shrivelled into his face. 'Trent? Nah, I had nothing to do with him.'

She took out her notebook. 'That's funny, Billy, because we have several eyewitness reports of you and Jack fighting in the pub last week.'

He downed the can of beer and stared at her. 'That was a mistake, that's all.'

Erasmus wiped the dust from the top of the TV. 'What was the fight about?'

Robinson shrunk into the sofa. 'Nothing.'

Erasmus laughed. 'So, you're coming to the station with us to continue this conversation?'

Jane Watson went to her partner and slapped him on the head.

'Hey! What's that for?'

She scowled at him. 'Just tell them, Billy, ya daft twat.'

Robinson rubbed at the mark on his skin. 'Okay, okay.' He dropped the beer can into a pile of others on the carpet. 'I owed him money I don't have. So he got nasty about it.'

'Money for what?' Erasmus said.

'If I tell you, they'll hurt me.'

Erasmus recognised the fear in his voice. 'Who will?'

Robinson lit another cigarette. 'I'll say, only if you promise it goes no further than this room.'

'We can't guarantee you anything,' Teo said.

Erasmus slapped his hand on the TV, and dust flew everywhere.

'I promise you this, Billy. If you don't spill your guts right now, I'll march over to that pub and tell everyone you've been singing like a canary.'

Robinson didn't take long to think about it. 'There's a new gang working the town, even into Boro and East Cleveland. I borrowed money from them through Jack. That's what the fight was about.'

'The daft twat lost it all on the nags again,' Jane Watson said.

Erasmus ignored her. 'What are the gang dealing in, Billy?'

A shadow crept over his face. 'Drugs mainly. They use kids to move the stuff around.'

'County lines,' Teo said.

'Do you have any names in this gang?' Erasmus asked.

Robinson sucked on his cigarette and filled the room

with smoke. It slipped into Erasmus's mouth and dived into his lungs, sparking a vivid memory of the last time he'd smoked – the day before going to Redlands when the drink and drugs had threatened to overwhelm him.

'David Miller is the main man in Redcar.'

Teo scribbled the name in her notebook. 'And where will we find him?'

'He's in The Dragon most nights. It's a new trendy pub on the seafront.'

'I know where it is,' Erasmus said. 'What does he look like?'

Robinson laughed. 'You can't miss him – he has an eyepatch like a pirate.'

'That seems appropriate for a drug dealer,' Teo said.

Erasmus loomed over Billy. 'Was Amy one of the kids this gang used to move the drugs over county lines?'

'What?' Jane Watson said.

Robinson's whole body shook. 'No, never.'

Erasmus glared at him. 'If I find out you were involved in Amy's disappearance, your life won't be worth living.'

He turned from him and left the house, his hands shaking as he got outside. The cigarette smoke lingered in his lungs, begging Erasmus to return to the fold. The air shimmered before him, and he would have sworn he heard Amy Watson calling his name.

'Erasmus? Erasmus, can you hear me?'

He blinked several times before his vision returned to normal, seeing Teo looking at him with concern.

'Do you still want to visit where Amy was last seen?'

She nodded. 'Yes. Then we'll visit this pub to find David Miller.'

They went to the car, and Erasmus directed her to the woods. They parked, and he led her into the trees.

'There are several ways in and out,' Erasmus said. 'Including another road on the other side of the wood. It's more secluded than where we came in.'

Teo scrutinised the area. 'Somebody could have snatched Amy and bundled her into a vehicle.'

'That was the most likely scenario the investigation arrived at. But we had no evidence for it or any eyewitnesses.'

'Do you think Robinson could have forced her into moving drugs for this gang he mentioned?'

'I wouldn't put anything past that scumbag.'

'Okay,' she said. 'So what next?'

Erasmus touched the pill bottle in his pocket. 'Let's go to the pub.'

Teo glanced at her watch. 'It's too early, Erasmus. If you want to find Miller there, it would be best to go later. We should update the others.'

He didn't mention thinking more of having a drink than finding the drug dealer with the eyepatch.

She drove to the station. 'Will you tell Beckett about the Amy Watson connection to our case?'

Erasmus shook his head. 'Is it a link to Amy or to Robinson?'

She narrowed her eyes. 'It's both, Erasmus.'

They exited the car and entered the building, finding the three DSs in the Murder Room. Erasmus told them what they'd discovered at the Watson house.

'Teo and I will visit The Dragon pub undercover to check on the man with the eye patch.' He looked at DS Black. 'Mel, see if Miller has a record and search for him online.'

Teo frowned. 'Undercover?'

Erasmus put his hands in his pockets and flexed his fingers thirteen times.

'We won't get anything out of him if we look like plain clothes coppers. Casual, pub-going attire should do the trick.'

She continued frowning. 'And if that doesn't work?'

His grin made Erasmus's jaw hurt. 'Then we find an excuse to arrest him.' He turned back to Black. 'Any luck with the online search for Trent and Robinson?'

DS Black swung her chair around to face everybody. 'There's no social media footprint for Trent and no internet presence. Robinson is the opposite. He's all over the world wide web with accounts on Facebook, Twitter, Instagram, YouTube and TikTok.'

Erasmus's heart leapt a beat. 'Did you get anything useful?'

Black shook her head. 'Not so far. I've only had time to go back twelve months, and all his posts are about football or horse racing. But I'll keep looking.'

It was frustrating news, but it gave him an idea. 'During the investigation into Amy Watson's disappearance, the cybercrime unit checked her mobile phone and computer, searching for anything unusual in her internet accounts.'

'You thought somebody might have groomed her online?' Teo said.

Erasmus nodded. 'It was a strong possibility, but we found nothing. I think it's worthwhile looking into it again with fresh eyes.' He looked at Black. 'Can you do that as well, Mel?'

'Of course, boss.'

He turned to Rankin and Kane. 'Any luck with the locals in the pub?'

DS Kane flicked through his notebook. 'Plenty. Several

regulars told us they'd seen Trent and Robinson together in the last few months.'

Rankin continued. 'But they always appeared friendly, laughing and joking, until that fight. Nobody knew what it was about.'

Erasmus processed the new information. 'Okay, excellent work everybody. We'll go over our next moves when we return tomorrow morning. Hopefully, Teo and I will have something useful from our excursions tonight.'

The team packed up as Teo sidled over to him. 'Are you sure about this?'

He gripped the bottle of pills in his pocket. 'You don't have to come. I can handle it myself.'

She laughed. 'What, and miss another session in the pub with you? I remember what happened the other night. Do you?'

He moved to the door. 'No drinking tonight, DS Andreescu.'

Well, perhaps one.

Chapter 30

The Dragon

Teo was opposite the pub by eight o'clock, standing near the sea wall and peering across the road, clutching her mobile phone.

I've put this off too long, so I might as well get it over with.

She dialled the number, and it was answered immediately.

'Where have you been, Teodora? You know I need that money.'

Teo calmed her racing heart. Not that she resented giving her mother the cash. It was more about not trusting her.

'How much do you want, Mum?'

'Two thousand pounds, Teodora. It will cover the bills for the next few weeks. I'll pay you back, I promise.'

It was less than Teo had expected, but she also assumed it wouldn't be the last time.

'Have you spoken to Dad about it?'

Daniela Andreescu snorted down the phone. 'Your

father is too busy with his teenage tart to bother about me and my problems.'

Six months ago, Florin Andreescu had left his wife for an eighteen-year-old dancer. Teo had never met the girl, though she'd had several heated conversations with him about it. All she knew about *Madison* was that she was five years younger than Teo and twenty-seven years younger than her father.

'It's his dad's money, Mum. I can't give you some of it without telling him.'

There was more snorting down the phone, and she wondered if her mother had acquired a pet pig.

'It's your money, Teodora; your inheritance. It's nothing to do with Florin. If Cristian had wanted his son to have it, he would have given it to him. But he knew Florian didn't deserve it, so he left it to you.'

I'm sure Grandfather wouldn't want you to have any either.

'Okay, I'll transfer it to your bank when I get home.'

There was a deep sigh down the line. 'Where are you, Teodora? Are you on a date?'

Yes, Mum, with my boss, who's twice my age and who I'm trying to keep an eye on to ensure he doesn't make himself ill.

'No, Mum, it's only a night out with the girls.'

Her mother's laughter made the phone vibrate in her hands.

'Ah, I remember those nights – so much better than wasting your time with men who only want one thing.'

'Sometimes women want that one thing as well, Mum.'

'Teodora! Don't be so smutty.'

The chance would be a fine thing. I haven't even kissed anybody in six months.

'Okay, Mum. I'll speak to you tomorrow. Bye.'

She ended the call before her mother could give her an extended lesson on behaving correctly.

Teo texted Bukowski. *What time are you getting here?*

'I could have murdered you by now.'

She spun around to see him standing near her, resting one hand on the fishing boat behind him. He tried to hide it, but she saw him tapping on the wood several times before he stopped.

'Do you say that to all the young women you sneak up on?'

He laughed. 'Just the clever ones.'

Teo scrutinised his clothes. 'You're wearing the same things as the other night.'

Erasmus shrugged. 'I thought they'd help me fit in with the crowd.'

'Have you washed them since last time?'

'Should I have?'

She cringed and waved one hand in front of her nose. 'Don't get too close to me.'

He pointed at the people entering the pub. 'I doubt it'll matter in there. It looks like it's heaving.'

Teo gulped down a blast of sea air and peered across the road at the punters.

'What do we do when we get inside?'

Erasmus rubbed at a stain on his Hex Pistols t-shirt.

'We'll split up and check the place, not just looking for David Miller but seeing if any other illegal activity is happening.'

'You want to make your first arrests since returning to work?'

'Not particularly, no. But if we spot something criminal, we can always hold it over the head of the bar manager so they'll tell us what they know about Miller.'

She scrutinised his face and knew he wasn't telling her everything.

'And what do we do if we see Miller inside?'

'Play it by ear.' He showed her his phone. 'We keep in touch regularly by text.'

'What do you hope to get out of tonight, Erasmus?'

'It's simple. First, we locate Miller and, if possible, follow him to wherever he lives. Then we can interview him there.'

'You don't want to question him here?'

He shrugged. 'Maybe, but we'd have to get him away from the pub.'

She heard the music booming opposite them, some drum and bass tune that made her ears twitch.

'Are you drinking tonight?'

Erasmus grinned at her. 'We have to blend in, Teo.'

He left her there, walked across the road, and pushed his way into the pub. She didn't move, feeling the wind against her face and smelling the saltwater.

Should I tell Beckett about this?

She'd expected the chief constable to contact her, asking if anything had happened between his niece and Darren Carter.

He hadn't, but she saw Carter walk into The Dragon as she thought about it.

Shit! What do I do now?

Teo got her phone ready to text Bukowski and call the whole thing off, but she knew he wouldn't leave that pub until he got what he wanted.

She couldn't abandon him in there alone, even with Carter in the pub.

Teo clenched her fists and crossed the road.

It was going to be a bumpy night.

Chapter 31

The Music

The noise and the smell hit Erasmus as he strode inside: the sound of some modern dance tune murdering Bowie's "Fame" bouncing off the walls, clinging with the aroma of fresh sweat. He headed straight to the bar, bumping elbows with people twenty years younger than him.

'A bottle of Corona,' he said to the miserable-looking bartender. 'And don't forget the lime.'

Erasmus paid for the drink with his debit card and moved from the hive as Teo entered insanity. He didn't look at her and wormed his way through the revellers, searching for the man with the eyepatch.

Maybe Robinson lied about that. If he were that scared of this gang, he wouldn't be worried about what the police would do to him.

Shoulders and hips bumped into him like a human dodgem, moving him to the side and not in his desired direction. He found a gap in the crowd and leaned against the wall, gulping his drink. The lime added to the taste of the booze, and warmth flowed through him. He scrutinised the punters, but there was no sign of Miller. He couldn't see Teo either, but he wasn't worried. She could look after herself. As Erasmus sipped the beer, only one name possessed his thoughts.

Amy Watson.

Could there be a connection between her disappearance and Jack Trent's murder? Was it possible this unknown county lines criminal organisation had used Amy, and they were the reason she vanished? Amy's stepfather claimed he owed the gang money, and Trent was the enforcer who sent him a message. And David Miller worked for this gang.

He made a mental note to call his contact at the National Crime Agency in the morning. They monitored organised crime across the UK and would be the ones likeliest to know anything about Miller.

'I love your T-shirt.'

Her voice rocked him back into the present, staring at a dark-haired woman older than most of the clientele in The Dragon. Not as old as him, but not far off. Her blue eyes sparkled like a Caribbean ocean, and she smelt of strawberries.

'They're a local band,' he said.

She smiled and nodded. 'I know. I saw them playing live the other night.'

He fought the urge to flex his fingers. 'At The Crown? I was at that gig.'

Her smile grew bigger. 'How fantastic were they?'

'Super fantastic.' He knew it sounded stupid as soon as the words came out of his mouth, but he couldn't stop himself.

The crowd grew and pushed her closer to him. 'I haven't seen you in here before.'

He took a long drink. 'I've been away for a while.'

She pressed her legs against his, and a volcano consumed his chest. 'I'm Emma.'

The pounding of his heart filled his skull. 'Erasmus.'

'Beloved,' she said.

The music increased in volume, and his ears vibrated. 'What?'

'Erasmus. It comes from the Greek meaning "beloved."'

'My mother picked it. My father always hated it.'

She was pinned to him now, her lips close to his cheek. 'She made a good choice.'

He said the first thing in his head. 'Are you local?'

Emma nodded. 'Born and bred in Redcar. There's nowhere I'd rather be than here, with the beautiful coast and countryside. How about you?'

'I'm from Middlesbrough and moved here as a kid. I've lived in other places, but I guess this is where I'm supposed to be.' And he still had a job to do. 'Are you a regular here?'

'Usually on the weekend, but tonight's a special occasion.'

Her perfume raced up his nose and overwhelmed his senses. 'What's that?'

Somebody bumped into her, and she grabbed his waist. Then she pointed in the direction where the music was coming from.

'It's the DJ's birthday.'

Her hand on him forced his heart to race even faster, but seeing the man playing the tunes focused his attention: he was wearing an eyepatch.

'Is that David Miller?'

Emma gripped him harder. 'Yes. Do you know him?'

'Only through the grapevine. Is he a friend of yours?'

She shook her head. 'No, but we hang around with

some of the same people. He travels all over the northeast with his music.'

Well, it's not quite his music. And travelling around the area as a DJ must be a good way of moving drugs between the counties.

'Will he be playing all night?'

'No,' she said. 'He'll be here for an hour; then there's a party at his place in Saltburn.'

Competing strands of excitement sped through him. 'Are you invited?'

'I might be. Would you like to come along?'

He tried to hide his eagerness. 'Sure, but let me get you a drink first.'

She pushed her face into his. 'I'll have Prosecco, please.'

Erasmus unlocked himself from her and pushed through the customers. He got to the bar and wiped the sweat from his head, ordering two drinks. His phone pinged as he waited. He slipped it out of his pocket and read the text.

Are you having a good time squashed against that woman?

The drinks arrived as he replied.

I had no way out.

He drank some Corona to cool down.

Yet somehow, you made it to the bar. Is the Prosecco for you?

Erasmus glanced around him, searching for Teo, but couldn't find her.

Where are you?

Near the DJ. Guess what I've found?

A pirate is spinning the records.

Nobody plays records anymore, doofus. They're all digital tunes. And yes, I'm staring at David Miller.

He sipped his drink, wondering if Emma would still be there when he returned. Teo sent another message.

And guess what?

What?

I've got an invitation to his place for a birthday party tonight.

Erasmus laughed inside.

That makes two of us. So I'll see you there.

He put the phone into his pocket and went looking for Emma.

Chapter 32

The DJ

Teo watched Bukowski leave the bar and fight through the mob to find his lady friend. Then she glanced across at her new acquaintance playing the tunes. It hadn't been challenging to worm her way into his affections, just a flutter of eyelashes and a few breathless words telling Miller how much she loved his music. The invitation to his birthday party soon followed.

'Do you want a drink?' he shouted at her over the noise.

She refused. 'I'm saving myself for later.' Teo knew from first-hand experience not to trust a stranger bringing her drinks.

The mobile phone was still in her grip when she got another message. She expected Erasmus to text her again, probably bragging about how well his night was going, but it was from her mother.

Don't forget the money, Teodora.

Teodora.

Dora. That's what she'd told Miller to call her, even though she hated it more than her birth name.

Dora, Dora, the monkey explorer, the kids had called her

at school. She never understood the monkey bit until she realised they meant it as an insult because she had foreign blood in her veins.

She didn't tell her parents about the name-calling and the bullying, putting up with it until she turned thirteen, and Annie's disappearance taught her there were worse things in the world than a few nasty names. Once she broke the biggest boy's fingers, nobody bothered her after that.

Teo peered through the crowd but had lost sight of Erasmus.

He shouldn't be drinking if we're working.

She hadn't worried about him at the gig, but her concerns had grown since then. She'd lied to him about there being no rumours at the station regarding his stay at Redlands. Teo had ignored those, yet there were some things she couldn't overlook. Several people, including DCI Brennan, had told her they'd noticed how Bukowski's fingers had trembled before he retreated from work. And she'd seen the same thing more than once over the last few days, getting more frequent once he'd heard Amy Watson's name.

I should talk to him about it.

She hadn't known him long, yet an unexpected bond had grown after the night at the gig. And she felt close to him when they climbed up to the cliffs, searching for where his father's body had lain undiscovered for five years. And she guessed he had no other friends at the station.

What happened between him and Brennan?

As she pondered that question, somebody grabbed her arm and pulled Teo away from the DJ booth. She formed her hand into a fist and turned, ready to smash the assailant in the face but stopping when she saw who it was.

'Are you following me?' Carter's eyes burned with

something more than irritation, his behaviour fuelled by chemical diesel and gasoline. 'I haven't been near the girl since you warned me off.'

She wriggled out of his grasp, feeling a bruise forming on her arm.

'I could arrest you for assault, Darren.'

The fire subsided in his pupils, the apologies falling from his lips quicker than a politician breaking their promises.

'I'm sorry, I'm sorry.' He held up his hands. 'I've had a shit day.'

'Do you want me to make it worse for you?'

'No, no, I said I was sorry.'

She dragged him into the shadows. 'Did you supply Phoebe with drugs?'

'Only a bit of dope. She wanted stronger stuff, but I can't get that.'

'What stronger stuff?'

His lips bounced up and down like butterfly wings. 'Ecstasy. Coke.'

Shit! How do I tell Beckett that?

'If not you, who supplies those?'

His mouth stopped quivering as he nodded at the DJ. 'You never heard it from me.'

Teo glanced at Miller, seeing him talking to a bearded man.

'Who's the bloke with him?'

'That's his brother, George.'

She inched closer to Carter, smelling whisky on his breath. 'Do you know who Miller works for?'

He threw up his hands and backed away. 'I never saw you.'

Then he slipped into the crowd, and she heard somebody shouting a name. It took her a second to realise it was hers.

'Dora, come on. It's time to go.'

Miller was beckoning her towards him, so she went. 'Is it party time?'

He grinned like the Cheshire Cat. 'It sure is. We'll slip out the back to avoid the punters.'

Before she could get her phone to text Bukowski, Miller grabbed her arm and pulled her through an exit. She stumbled into an alley, standing on discarded pizza boxes and empty beer cans. It smelt of dog shit, and a broken street light flickered above her.

Teo held up her hand to protect her eyes. 'Are we getting a taxi?'

'You're getting something,' Miller said before slamming her against a wall and pushing a knife to her throat.

'What?' she said.

'Who are you working for?' he said. 'Is it the Geordies?'

The blade kissed her flesh. 'Don't be stupid, David. You'll get locked up for this.'

He glanced around the alley before returning his focus to her.

'The people I work for can make anyone disappear.'

The crumbling brickwork cut into her back. 'And who's that?'

Before he could reply, she heard a roar from the pub, turning her head to see Erasmus running towards them. Only he wasn't running but stumbling, his legs going in opposite directions as he hit a crate and crashed to the ground. The distraction was enough to bring her arm up and into Miller's Adam's apple. He dropped the knife and clutched his throat. Then, for good measure, she kneed him in the balls.

Teo wiped the blood from her neck and peered at the groaning DJ.

'Here's your gift from Dora.' She showed him her warrant card. 'You're nicked.'

She knew she'd have to tell him the required legal words for an arrest, but she needed to take a breath first.

Then she realised Erasmus was unconscious.

Chapter 33

The Terror

Flashing lights and sirens assaulted Erasmus's senses, a cacophony and vision swirling in his head. He'd gone looking for Teo, sensing she was in danger, but his world had changed. There was no sign of her or the DJ. Instead, bodies littered the ground, victims calling for help, crying out for their loved ones. Police officers were helping the wounded, rushing past him in a haze of confusion and terror. Then he heard the gunshots above him. Sobbing, yelling, and wailing. A bullet nipped his fingers. Blood on the ground. Lots of blood. Not his.

People screamed, the smell of death in his nostrils and the taste of decay on his lips. He looked around him, and it wasn't Redcar anymore. The pub had disappeared, and he saw the River Thames nearby. The terror surrounded him. A smartly dressed young woman in a navy blue suit lay before him, her guts spilling onto the pavement. Men, women, and children rushed everywhere in the chaos. A giant of a man wielding an axe sprinted towards him, raising the blade to decapitate him. Then the shot rang out. It entered the man's forehead, exploding from the other

245

side, taking blood and bone. He crashed next to Erasmus, a great oak felled in a forest. His eyes were open, his mouth moving, spewing filth and hate. He was dying, but Erasmus leaned forward and put his hands around that thick neck, squeezing the throat like a ripe tomato. He didn't know how long he stayed like that, only relinquishing dead flesh when a uniformed police officer pulled him away.

Then he blacked out.

And he slept.

Erasmus heard voices, a man and a woman, people he recognised. His eyes flickered open, and his vision blurred. He lay in a hospital bed, the sounds transforming into the occasional clear words.

'He saved many lives.'

'He's lost a lot of blood.'

'He'll survive.'

Then they disappeared, and all he heard were hushed whispers. His view was still half in reality and half in slumber. He knew it was only a dream, confirmed when his eyesight cleared, and he stared across the room to see his father holding his mother. They were both wearing hospital uniforms, but he understood it was only another of his hallucinations when his father said something impossible to his mother.

'I love you.'

She pushed him away. 'I don't love you, James. I never did.'

The two of them shimmered in front of Erasmus, clinging to his hallucination, and he knew his mind was finally processing what his mother had told him. She'd had an affair with her husband's brother before and after her marriage: an uncle who might be his father.

'You're not who you said you were,' Erasmus said in his fevered state.

Then, the darkness returned.

He was still in the hospital bed when he woke.

'Finally, the Kraken awakes.'

Erasmus pushed his back up and rubbed the sleep from his face. 'What are you doing here, Bella?'

Dr Toon grinned at him. 'You're two floors above the mortuary. I could sense you were here when they brought you in.'

His skull ached, and he touched his forehead, finding a plaster. 'What happened to me?'

'You ran into the alley behind The Dragon, straight into an empty crate, falling and hitting your head on the wall. You should sue the owners for violations of health and safety.'

He smiled at the sound of Teo's voice as she entered the room.

'Are you okay?' he asked.

'Me? I'm fine. You're the one in the hospital bed.'

Bella Toon interrupted them. 'We'll, you're clearly okay, and I've got people to cut up. So I'll talk later, Erasmus.' He was about to speak when she stopped in the doorway. 'Oh, there was another reason I came to see you. I was wrong about Jack Trent.'

'Wrong?' Teo said.

'Yes,' Bella replied. 'It wasn't the train that killed Kent. He was already dead when it hit him. I suppose that was a small mercy.'

Erasmus sat up in bed. 'So what killed him?'

'Do you remember the undigested crab found in his stomach?' Erasmus and Teo nodded together. 'He choked on that.'

'Shit!' Teo said. 'How long before he reached the train tracks would it have happened?'

Bella shrugged. 'It's impossible to tell, but if we add the crab to the ketamine we discovered in his system, you can make an obvious assumption.'

Erasmus ignored the pain shooting through his face and neck.

'Somebody drugged Kent to make him pliable, then forced the crab down his throat before pushing him in front of that train.'

Teo shook her head. 'That's a convoluted way to kill someone.'

'It's unusual,' Toon said, 'but I've seen plenty of strange murder weapons: a woman who was choked after her husband shoved a crucifix into her mouth; a man decapitated with a guitar string; and a bloke bludgeoned to death with a frozen leg of lamb.'

'Still,' he said. 'Murder by crab?'

Bella grinned. 'And the more unusual thing is that the crab isn't even native to this area.'

Erasmus rubbed at his forehead, wondering if he was still hallucinating. 'Where, then?'

'It was a Chinese mitten crab,' Bella said. 'It's native to East Asia's rivers, estuaries, and other coastal habitats from Korea in the north to Fujian, China in the south. It's also been introduced to Europe and North America, where it's considered an invasive species. This means the import and trade of the species are forbidden in the whole EU.'

Teo laughed. 'Yeah, but we're not part of that club

anymore.' She looked at her phone. 'Mitten crabs were first discovered in England over seventy years ago, and it's thought they were accidentally transported here in the ballast of ships.'

'Why would somebody kill Kent like this?' he asked.

'That's a mystery for you to solve,' Bella said. 'Make sure you don't eat any strange crustaceans when you leave here, Erasmus.'

She left, and Teo moved to the bed. 'What if the killer intended it to be a message?'

The hospital gown irritated Erasmus's skin. 'What message? And who was it for?'

Teo took the empty seat next to him. 'If Kent was working for a county lines drug gang, perhaps they had him killed as a warning to one of their competitors.'

'Why choke him using a Chinese crab?'

Teo crossed her legs. 'Who knows how the criminal mind works?'

'Speaking of criminals,' he said, 'what happened in that alley?'

She smiled at him. 'You mean after you knocked yourself out?'

He touched the back of his neck. 'Yeah, I thought I was helping you.'

'You did. Your kamikaze act distracted Miller enough for me to kick him in the balls.'

He grimaced. 'Ouch! Then what transpired?

'I arrested him and called an ambulance for you. Which is why you're in that bed.'

'And Miller?'

She sighed. 'We could only charge him with the assault on me, so he's already out on bail. He kept silent whenever asked about drug dealing and who he might work for.'

The pain in Erasmus's head increased. 'So it was all for nothing?'

She pointed at his hand. 'I wouldn't say that.'

Erasmus looked at his palm, reading the name and phone number written there.

'Emma. I'd forgotten about her.'

Teo laughed. 'Yeah, right?' She uncrossed her legs and leaned closer to him. 'But speaking of forgotten things. I've sat here for hours since they brought you in and ....'

He returned her smile. 'And I owe you a drink.'

'It's not that. You were talking in your sleep.'

'Damn. I hope I didn't swear too much.'

'What happened to you in London, Erasmus?'

He looked at Teo, knowing he couldn't keep it from her.

'Several years ago, I was on holiday in London when two men attacked random people. One had a pistol; the other had an axe. I helped the police stop that attack. That's all it was.'

'That's all? It sounded traumatic.'

He suddenly wanted to tell her some of the thoughts that burdened him. 'In my first year as a copper, I saw a young mother, eight-and-a-half-months pregnant, inject herself with heroin because her craving for smack was more potent than her love for her unborn child. The baby became a junkie, too, quivering inside her stomach for the drug. So when it was born, the first thing that happened was it was put on baby methadone. It was one of those things you see with your own eyes and cannot believe and never forget.' He let the memories wash through him. 'You never become accustomed to managing the sorrow of those near the victims, but you learn to handle your emotions in front of them and everyone else, storing the agony for a hopefully more appropriate time. But there's a different type of situation to handle when dealing with victims of crimes – when they have nobody to grieve for them. An old woman, the victim of a violent robbery, with nobody to care for her. The young man, orphaned at an early age, who could never make friends, killed by a stranger's punch. The lonely woman, whose work colleagues ridiculed her, murdered on her way home by a drunk. I've encountered those and many others over the years.' He tapped the side of his head. 'You try to keep the memories out of here, but it's impossible. So you store them in the shadows, and if they creep out, you use something else as a distraction: booze, drugs, sex, or anything that works for you. And when someone like me does that, with my condition, it's just asking for trouble.'

Teo peered into his eyes. 'But, with help from the Redlands staff, you survived all that. You're better now.'

'Yes, but I'm concerned that one thing could tip me over the edge again.'

'Amy Watson?' she said.

He nodded. 'As soon as we made that connection between Kent and Amy's stepfather, I hoped we might finally discover what happened to her. And now, if we don't, I'm unsure I could handle it.'

Teo reached out and held his hand. 'I'll help you, Erasmus. And you have other friends as well – Sapphy and the rest of The Hex Pistols. After the other night, they're your mates for life.'

Her touch made him feel human for the first time in ages. 'I didn't embarrass myself?'

She laughed. 'Of course you did. That's why they're all our best friends now.'

A man entered the room. 'Don't overexcite him, DS Andreescu. He'll be going home in a few hours.'

Teo turned to him. 'Laughter is the best medicine, Dr Roberts.'

Roberts approached him. 'How are you feeling, Inspector Bukowski?'

Erasmus sat up straight. 'Great, Doc. I'm ready to go now.'

Roberts looked at his head. 'It seems it was only a mild concussion, but perhaps you should take a few days off from work. And if you feel any pain or headaches, contact us immediately.'

He left without another word, and Erasmus turned to Teo.

'Okay, partner, I've one last important question for you.'

'What's that?' she said.

He got out of bed. 'Where are my clothes?'

Chapter 34

The Past

A cloudless ocean-blue sky greeted Erasmus as he stepped out of the hospital. A group of smokers were standing opposite, chugging on nicotine while berating the state of the NHS. Teo shook her car keys at him.

'I'll take you home.'

He rubbed at his stomach as it groaned. 'I'm starving.'

'Is that a hint you want me to cook for you?'

'Can you cook?'

'I'll have you know, Detective Inspector Bukowski, that I'm an excellent cook. Are you a vegetarian?'

He shook his head. 'A former girlfriend converted me several years ago, but it didn't last.'

'The relationship or the vegetarianism?'

'Both.'

'Okay. I can make you some traditional Romanian dishes my grandfather taught me: mici followed by Ciorbă de burtă. That's grilled minced meat rolls and beef tripe soup.'

An invisible entity clawed at his guts. 'That sounds

fantastic, Teo, and I'd love to try those someday, but I need to eat something in the next fifteen minutes, or I'm going to collapse.'

'Well, we can't have that. So what do you suggest?'

He pointed at the pub across the road. 'They do decent food. Let's go there, and we can talk about the case.'

She didn't argue, taking the short distance to the boozer. Once inside, Teo found a table while Erasmus went to the bar. Then he joined her, with cider for him and white wine for her.

He sat at the table. 'Only a small glass for you since you're driving.'

'Should you be drinking straight out of the hospital?'

He took a large gulp, letting the sweetness stimulate the back of his throat.

'One pint won't hurt me.' He grabbed a menu and flicked through it. 'Steak and chips for me.' He handed it to her. 'What about you?'

She scrutinised the offerings of pub grub. 'It's too late for Sunday lunch, so I'll have their chicken pasta.'

Erasmus took his phone from his pocket. 'Great. I owe you, so it's my treat. I'll order through the app.'

Teo took a sip of her wine. 'What did people do before mobile phones and the internet?'

'They survived,' he said. 'We have more access to technology than our parents or grandparents did, but it doesn't mean this world is any better or worse. Just different.'

'You don't think technology has given more opportunity for criminals and the hateful to pursue their terrible ways?'

He took another drink of cider. 'The hateful?'

'You know what I mean, Erasmus. The bigots, and racists, and misogynists, and fascists – they all have louder voices than at any time since the 1930s.'

'If you support free speech, you tolerate things you may disagree with, even if they may cause harm to others.'

She smiled at him. 'Who said I believe in free speech?'

He was surprised at her words. 'You don't?'

'Free speech doesn't mean free from consequences. For example, you wouldn't allow a sex offender to stand outside a school and tell the world their views. So why would you permit somebody to spout things that might get others killed or hurt?'

'That's why we have laws against that, Teo. You know this.'

A server wearing a bright green shirt brought their food to them. Erasmus stuck a handful of chips into his mouth to ease the aching in the pit of his stomach.

'My paternal great-grandfather was a member of the Romania Iron Guard, a militant revolutionary fascist movement and political party. It existed in the early part of the Second World War when it came to power. Members were called Legionnaires or Greenshirts because of their predominantly green uniforms. When Marshal Ion Antonescu assumed control in September 1940, he brought the Iron Guard into the government, creating the National Legionary State. In January 1941, following the Legionnaires' rebellion, Antonescu used the army to suppress the movement, destroying the organisation; its commander, Horia Sima, and other leaders escaped to Germany. My great-grandfather disappeared, but my great-grandmother fled to England, where she gave birth to my grandfather. When I was a kid, I'd sit in the living room listening to him telling stories of how they escaped from Romania and their struggles in this country as refugees.' She glanced through the bar, hearing the latest news of those dying in the English Channel as they sought safety from another war. 'I sometimes wonder just how civilised we are as a society.'

Erasmus fiddled with his glass. 'Are you close to your parents?'

'More with my mother than father. They divorced the year I joined the force, and I saw less of them once I left home. How about you?'

He took a deep breath. 'My father was always a workaholic, having little time for my mother and me. She didn't need to work with his salary, but she was easily bored, so she got a part-time job in our local community centre when I was deemed old enough to look after myself.'

'When was that?'

'I was ten, so it was the summer of 1993.' Darkness seeped out of his eyes. 'That's when I started noticing something wrong with her.' He swallowed a piece of steak, which felt like steel as it dropped into his gut. 'I'd see her talking to people who weren't there, having conversations with herself.'

'You think she was hallucinating?'

'I guess so.'

'Early signs of dementia?'

Erasmus shrugged. 'She was thirty then, but I suppose it's possible. My dad arranged regular visits to hospitals and doctors through his contacts. Sometimes, she stayed away for one or two nights, and I was left with the neighbours to look after me while my father cut people open. When she was home, she tried hard to be normal, and I just accepted things as they were. Then, as I got into my teens, I knew she was ill and her memory was failing. She'd forget where stuff was or struggle with people's names.'

'Could she have had bipolar disorder?'

'Bipolar disorder might be linked to genetics, as it seems

to run in families. The family members of a person with it have an increased risk of developing it themselves. But no single gene is responsible for bipolar disorder.' He took a deep breath. 'Eventually, it became impossible for my mother to do things around the house, so my father employed a woman to help.' He pushed the glass away from him. 'I came home from school early one day and caught him with her in my bedroom. He shouted at me and told me to play with my friends.'

Teo grimaced. 'Where was your mum?'

Erasmus's laugh wasn't of happiness. 'He'd arranged for her to see a memory specialist. How convenient was that?'

'Do you think she knew about his infidelity?'

'Well, there was more than one woman, so I guess she must have.' He drank more than half of the cider, eating as he went. 'But there were things about my mother I didn't know then.'

Teo scooped pasta into her mouth, talking as she ate. 'Such as?'

Erasmus peered into her eyes, wondering if he'd said too much already. But then he continued. 'When I visited her at the care home, she was as lucid as I'd seen her in decades. And she told me she'd had an affair with my uncle, my father's brother, before and after she married my father.'

A piece of pasta hung from Teo's lips like the condemned on the gallows.

'Christ. How do you feel about that?'

He shrugged. 'I don't know.'

'Where's this uncle now?'

Erasmus finished his steak. 'He died of a heart attack four years ago.'

She pushed her plate away with only half of it eaten. 'You were hallucinating in the hospital.'

'I was,' he said. 'I blame the bang on the head.'

Teo forced her lips into a grin. 'What did you see?'

'My father and mother, dressed as a doctor and nurse.'

'But she wasn't a nurse?'

'No. He never let her near the hospital when he was working. So, I don't know why I pictured her in a nurse's uniform. But he also told her he loved her, and I'd never seen or heard that before.'

'Do you think it was an early memory of yours from when you were a small child, now resurrected because of your recent experiences?'

He finished his cider and immediately craved more. 'I know nothing anymore, Teo. Inside my head, it's a constant swirl of confused mush.'

'Perhaps we should concentrate on the Trent investigation.'

He stood up. 'Sure, but I need another pint.'

Erasmus turned away, seeing her scowl. He went to the bar and ordered the cider. He didn't look at her while he waited, thinking about what had happened in the hospital.

That's the only time I've had hallucinations since leaving Redlands, and they only came after I'd banged my head. So there's nothing to worry about.

He returned to the table as she was writing in her notebook. She stopped as he sat.

'So, this is what we have so far: it looks like somebody murdered Jack Trent by forcing a Chinese crab into his throat. Then they pushed him in front of a train. Because of Trent's link to Billy Robinson, we assume Trent worked for an organised gang that moves drugs across county lines. Robinson informed us that David Miller, the DJ with an eyepatch, is one of the top suppliers for this criminal organisation. Is that about right?'

Erasmus watched the bubbles float to the top of his cider.

'We can't ignore the fact that Billy Robinson is the step-father of Amy Watson.' The agony in his heart resurfaced. 'And the one thing we're sure about with county lines gangs is they use children as couriers for their drugs. So maybe that's why she disappeared a year ago.'

'You think something might have gone wrong during a transaction, and Amy paid the price?'

Erasmus put his hands under the table and clenched his fists. 'If that's true, then Robinson and Miller would probably know about it.'

'You have doubts about that?' Teo said.

He nodded. 'For Robinson, yes. I interviewed him several times while investigating Amy's disappearance, and I never felt he was involved.'

'Okay. We still need to find the person who gave Trent the card we found in his work locker, the mysterious Steve who was renting that place in Loftus.' She drank more of her wine. 'And we might have another lead to pursue.'

Erasmus's eyelids flickered. 'Yeah?'

'In The Dragon pub, I saw David Miller in deep conversation with his brother, George. Maybe we can lean on him for information.'

'How do you know it was Miller's brother?'

'The DJ told me. I think that's when he became suspicious about me and put that knife against my throat in the alley.'

He glanced at the small mark on her neck. 'We might have another avenue to follow.'

'What?'

Erasmus got his phone and flicked through it. 'I have a

contact at the NCA. If county lines gangs are operating around here, she should know.'

'She?'

He dialled the number. 'Orla Zen is only a friend, nothing more. So don't start thinking she is.'

Teo laughed. 'Orla Zen? What sort of name is that?'

Erasmus stared at the screen. 'I guess a pretty unique one, DS Teodora Andreescu.'

She frowned at him. 'Did you look at my personal file at the station?'

He grinned at her. 'Always best to know who you're working with, Teo.'

The connection clicked on the other end of the line before she replied.

'How I've missed your voice, Bukowski.'

Erasmus beamed as he replied.

Chapter 35

The Drugs

Fifteen minutes later, Orla Zen joined them, clutching a Coke.

'She's an investigator at the Newcastle branch of the National Crime Agency,' Erasmus had told Teo once he'd ended the phone call with Zen.

'I'm sorry about your father, Erasmus. He was a good man.'

He peered at her through his pint glass before putting it on the table.

'I didn't know you'd met him, Orla.'

'Only once.' She bit into an ice cube. 'He was an expert witness in one of our cases.'

'Expert in what?' Teo said.

Zen narrowed her eyes at Teo. 'The NCA had located a human trafficking gang in the northeast who'd started an operation in illegal organ transplants. Dr Bukowski provided expert evidence on how the organs would be stored and transported out of the country.'

Erasmus glanced at the bit of steak left on his plate. 'Any organs in particular?'

'Kidneys mainly, but illegal liver transplants are on the rise now.'

He shook his head. 'My father never told me any of this.'

Zen sipped at her Coke. 'You said the two of you rarely spoke.'

He nodded. 'That's true.' He saw the impatience in Teo's eyes. 'But that's not why I asked you here.' He told her what they had in the Trent murder investigation. 'So we'd like to know if the NCA is investigating any organised crime gangs in Teesside, especially in Redcar.'

She smiled at him. 'Why do you think I'm staying in a cheap hotel in Middlesbrough?'

He laughed. 'I guessed you weren't here for the tourist sites.'

A server arrived to remove the plates from the table. Erasmus resisted the urge to order another pint of cider.

'What do you do in the NCA, Ms Zen?' Teo asked.

Orla Zen moved her Coke to the side. 'There is significant, often deadly, competition between rival organised crime groups at all stages of class A drug production and supply. Corruption thrives at every step of the drug supply chain, including using crooked port and airport officials. Opium production in Afghanistan and cocaine production in Colombia are at record levels. This increase has the added effect of a high level of drug purity on the street, as the criminals have less need to use cutting agents, which brings its own dangers. The chemicals necessary for amphetamine production continue to enter the country in volume while street prices drop, indicating rising availability. Organised crime groups engaged in drug trafficking are typically also involved in other criminal activities. The profits from illegal drugs fund various criminal operations, including buying illegal firearms and financing terrorism. So I'm just one cog in a chain trying to stop all this activity.'

'What about the county lines trade?' Erasmus said.

Zen stared at him. 'A recent NCA assessment suggests there are more than a thousand lines in operation nationally, where a typical line will generate near £2,000 to £3,000 per day.'

'No wonder it's popular,' Teo said.

Zen continued. 'Young people exploited in this way are usually trafficked to areas far from home as part of a gang's narcotics network. The gangs coax children into this illicit web in several ways, including approaching them outside school gates or using an older family member as an introduction. The initial concrete sign something is wrong is when they go missing – for hours and days at first, then for weeks and months at a time, and sometimes forever.' She inched closer to Erasmus. 'Is this connected to Amy Watson's disappearance?'

He told her about the connection between Jack Trent, Billy Robinson, and David Miller. 'Do you recognise any of those names?'

Zen nodded. 'Miller is well known to us. We're just waiting for him to slip up and provide the evidence connecting the drug trade to who we believe is the gang's leader.'

'Who's that?' he said.

She removed her mobile phone. 'If you weren't my friend, Erasmus, you know I wouldn't tell you this.'

'I'll owe you big time, Orla.'

Zen passed her phone to him. 'Memorise that information because I can't give you copies.'

He scrutinised the data before handing the mobile to Teo. 'Take photos of all of it.'

She did while he lowered his voice and spoke to Zen. 'Alex West, that's who you believe is running the crime gang?'

Zen drank her Coke before replying. 'You've heard of him.'

Teo answered. 'He's the proprietor of several pubs and restaurants in the area and his West Building and Construction company is situated on the industrial estate near the Freeport.'

'How convenient is that?' Zen said.

Erasmus saw the links connecting in his head. 'And he owns The Dragon pub.'

Teo returned the phone to Zen. 'Why do you think West is the gang leader?'

Zen put the mobile into her jacket. 'Several mid-level dealers have given us his name, but we have no direct evidence yet. The NCA cybercrime and financial units have poured through his accounts, but we still don't have enough to take to the Crown Prosecution Service.' She located a document on her phone and showed it to Erasmus. 'There's nothing unusual about his financial accounts. He spends most of his time at the gym or the tennis club.'

The wheels ticked over inside Erasmus's head. 'Jack Trent worked for the Border Force at the Freeport. So, let's say West had him murdered by somebody forcing a crab into his throat. Killing him like that had to be a message to anyone considering moving in on West's operation.' They nodded in agreement. 'Which would mean Trent must have contacted one of these rival gangs. So perhaps that contact was the mysterious "Steve" who sent him the card we found in his work locker.'

'So,' Teo said. 'All we have to do is find Steve.'

Zen finished her Coke. 'There's another thing. My

colleagues and I believe West has links abroad, particularly East Asia.'

Teo dropped her notebook on the table. 'That would explain using the Chinese mitten crab to kill Trent. But if that was to be a warning, and they pushed him in front of the train to destroy the evidence, how would anybody see that message?'

'Simple,' Erasmus said. 'They filmed the whole thing on a mobile phone.'

Orla Zen smiled at him. 'If you could find that video....'

He stopped thinking about having another pint of cider.

It would be gin and tonic time when he got home.

Chapter 36

The Confrontation

Erasmus arrived early at work on Monday. He grabbed a coffee and made his way to the Murder Room. It was empty, as was the one DCI Brennan and his team used. He stood outside the window, peering at the photos and documents pinned to the boards. Then he glanced behind him, seeing a deserted police station.

It's now or never.

He pushed the door open and walked inside. The mug warmed his hands as he studied the information.

'You shouldn't be in here, Erasmus.'

He didn't turn around. 'The person who found my father's remains wasn't a dog walker, Paul.'

DCI Brennan stood next to him. 'You should leave now, Inspector Bukowski.'

He turned to his former friend and saw the room filling up with Brennan's team. And he noticed Teo in the open doorway.

'Did you hear what I said, Paul?'

'Ted Rice was walking his whippet at the fanhouse near the old Huntcliff ironstone mine when his mutt ran into the bushes. He thought it was chasing a fox until he found your father's remains.'

Erasmus shook his head. 'Mr Rice lied to you. He was likely there for an illicit sexual encounter and couldn't tell you because the other person is married.'

DCI Brennan laughed loud enough to hurt Erasmus's ears. 'And how do you know this?'

Erasmus glanced at Teo in the doorway and guessed the worry he saw in her eyes was for him. He put the coffee on the table.

'You don't have a lot of details on these boards, Paul.' He pointed at two photos. 'I assume the pictures of my mother and me are because we're suspects.'

'So. you can't answer my question?' Brennan replied.

Teo pushed past the others and stood near Erasmus. 'Time to leave, Inspector Bukowski. You must update the team on what we discovered over the weekend.'

'You should listen to her, Erasmus,' Chief Constable Beckett said as he entered the room.

'Why do you think my father was halfway between Saltburn and Skinningrove on the cliffs, Sam? He wasn't a regular walker. And he never enjoyed being in the countryside.'

'You always walked that route,' Brennan answered.

Erasmus grinned at him. 'Sure, I did, Paul. And most of the time, I was with you. I don't see your photo on the board.'

'Be careful with what you say next, Inspector Bukowski,' Beckett warned.

Erasmus scrutinised the people in the room and saw only one friendly face.

'My father was a serial philanderer and cheated on my mother with numerous women. I believe he was at the spot to have sex when his latest partner killed him. So that's who you should search for: whoever was his last affair. Start with the staff at the hospital, especially Dr Marsh. He benefited from my father's death so he might know who his mistress was.'

DCI Brennan laughed again. 'Like father, like son, then?'

He stared at his former friend. 'There's no need to bring that up now, Paul.'

Brennan pushed him against the board. 'Oh, you don't want others to hear about that.'

'What's he talking about?' Teo said.

Beckett separated the two men. 'This is over, Erasmus. Go to my office.'

Brennan stood his ground. 'No, Sam. He wanted to travel this route, so let's finish it.' He turned to Teo. 'We were childhood friends, always looking out for each other. Did he tell you why that ended?'

She shook her head. 'No.'

'What a surprise.' Brennan addressed everybody. 'I meant it when I said like father, like son.' Then he pointed at Erasmus. 'How do you think I felt when I arrived home one night to find you fucking my wife?'

The combined gasp sucked all the air from the room, and Erasmus knew he deserved what was coming.

'I'm sorry, Paul. I wasn't in a good place then, but you didn't deserve that.'

Brennan thumped his hand against the board, and the photo of Amelia Bukowski fell to the floor. Erasmus retrieved the picture of his mother.

Chief Constable Beckett raised his voice. 'My office now, Bukowski.'

Erasmus slipped the picture of his mother into his

jacket pocket and followed Beckett out of the room, unable to look at Teo as he left.

The chief constable slammed the door behind them before sitting at his desk. Erasmus watched his cheeks turn orange and waited for him to calm down.

'Would you like to tell me what that was all about, Bukowski?'

Erasmus didn't take a seat. 'Eighteen months ago, I had an affair with Stella Brennan. It's no excuse, but my mind was all over the place then, and I thought I was going mad. I needed somebody to love me, and she did. Or at least she told me she did. Paul found out and left Stella. And he stopped talking to me.'

Beckett puffed out his red cheeks. 'Did this behaviour affect your police work?'

Erasmus shook his head. 'I don't think so.'

'Did it influence your decision to enter the Redlands Psychiatric Unit?'

'It was one influence amongst several, yes.'

Beckett stared at Erasmus for a minute. 'If you go anywhere near DCI Brennan's investigation again, I'll suspend you from active police work. Do you understand DI Bukowski?'

He nodded. 'Yes, sir.'

'Where are you at in the Trent investigation?'

Erasmus told him everything they'd discovered, including the link to Amy Watson and the conversation he and Teo had with Orla Zen.

The flame returned to Beckett's face. 'You contacted the NCA without my permission?'

'It was a matter of urgency, sir.'

He waited for the chief constable to explode, thankful when he didn't.

'Do you think Trent's death connects to Amy Watson's disappearance?'

'Trent and Robinson knowing each other tells me there must be a link.'

'So, what will you do now?' Beckett said.

'Bring Billy Robinson to the station. Try to track down the "Steve" who knew Trent and was staying in Loftus. And interview Alex West.'

Beckett rubbed at his chin. 'What reason have you for interviewing West?'

'I don't know yet, sir, but I'll find one.'

The chief constable opened the desk's top drawer and removed a packet of gum. He didn't offer Erasmus a piece.

'I want updates twice daily, do you understand?' Erasmus nodded. 'And stay away from DCI Brennan and all of his team.'

Erasmus left the room and wondered how many more mistakes he could make before Beckett kicked him off the investigation.

Chapter 37

The Update

The others were deep in conversation when Erasmus entered the room. He looked at them and assumed Teo had told them what happened with DCI Brennan. However, he didn't dwell on it, going to the boards and seeing the new photos of the Miller brothers and Alex West.

'Everyone is up to date,' Teo said.

He glanced between them, knowing they were waiting for him to lead.

'Mel and Ian – I need you to go through the Amy Watson files to see if there is any link to Jack Trent, the Millers, or Alex West. Martin, contact Border Force at the Freeport and ask them for the names of all their staff. If West runs an organised crime gang bringing drugs through the port, and Trent worked for them, they must have somebody else doing his job now.' Then he pointed at the image of David Miller. 'The DJ is the connection between Jack Trent and Alex West. If he won't talk to us, perhaps we should interview the brother.' He turned to Teo. 'What do we know about him?'

'George Miller, thirty-five years old. No criminal record and lives alone close to the hospital in Middlesbrough.'

Erasmus raised his eyebrows. 'The hospital?'

She nodded. 'He works there as a porter.'

'Could he be supplying West with stolen drugs from the hospital?' DS Rankin asked.

He shook his head. 'My father told me once how tight security is regarding the distribution and movement of medicines through the hospital. And even if George Miller had broken that somehow, the amount he'd need to steal to make it worthwhile to West would be noticed pretty quickly. So, no, I don't think the younger Miller is stealing from the hospital, but he might be selling drugs brought through the port like his brother. Remember, David Miller works as a DJ, travelling across the northeast and probably beyond. That would be an ideal way to move drugs around.'

'To go with their county lines operation?' DS Black said.

Erasmus agreed. 'According to my NCA contact, yes.'

'We should interview George Miller here,' Teo said.

'Perhaps,' Erasmus replied. 'Or we could speak to him at the hospital, let his colleagues know the police are interested in him. If we get nothing useful, we'll bring David to the station and drop hints George has told us everything.'

She crossed her arms. 'I'm not sure about that.'

He shrugged. 'Why not?'

'If we bring David Miller here, after what happened between him and me in that alley, he's likely to have his solicitor with him. Do you want to lie in front of him and on record?'

'It won't be a lie,' Erasmus said. 'Only an omission of the truth.'

Teo grabbed his arm and dragged him away from the others. 'What are you doing?'

He wriggled from her grasp. 'What I must, Teo, to catch a group of dangerous criminals. It's nothing illegal, just a flexible understanding of police procedure.'

She scowled at him. 'If you break PACE, we'll have no legal leg to stand on if the case goes to court.'

He smiled at her. 'Don't worry. The Police and Criminal Evidence Act will be fine in our hands.'

Her scowl increased. 'You can't mislead suspects, especially in front of their solicitors, because you're obsessed with finding Amy Watson.'

Erasmus shook his head. 'Wouldn't you do the same to discover what happened to Annie Hamilton?'

He watched her struggling to control the anger burning behind her eyes.

'That's a low blow, Erasmus, and you know it.'

He glanced at the rest of the team. 'Did you tell them about Brennan and me?'

'I had to,' she replied. 'They would have found out, anyway. So, it was better coming from me.' She glared at him. 'It would have been better from you.'

'You're right,' he said. He moved from her and went to the centre of the room. 'Okay, everybody, I need your attention for a second.' They stopped what they were doing and stared at him. 'You've undoubtedly heard about the events regarding DCI Brennan and me.' He glanced at Teo. 'It's all true, but the investigation into my father's murder won't interfere with our work here. Not anymore. Now, does anybody have any questions?'

They didn't and returned to their tasks. DS Black's phone rang, and she answered it as Teo spoke to Erasmus.

'Did you mean all that?'

'Don't you believe me?'

'It's not that, Erasmus, but you're worrying me.'

'You're worried my mania is returning?' He got the tablets from his jacket and removed the lid. 'Perhaps I should swallow a few of these to put both our minds at rest.'

She gazed at the medication in his palm. 'Do you think you need to take them?'

He stared at the pills, enjoying their texture against his skin. Then he replaced them in the bottle and returned it to his pocket.

'No, Teo, I don't. What I feel now isn't the same as what happened last year.' He nodded to the others working nearby. 'I'm full of adrenalin because I can see progress in the investigation. And yes, I was frustrated with what was happening – or not happening – regarding my father's murder, but that's passed. For all the problems between Paul and me, I know he's a damn good detective.'

DS Black stood up and spoke. 'That was the housing association finally returning my calls about the man they rented the house in Loftus to.'

'Jack Trent's mysterious friend "Steve"?' Teo said.

DS Black nodded. 'They gave me his name – Steve King.'

DS Kane laughed. 'Stephen King? Like the writer?'

'I doubt it's the same one,' DS Black replied, 'but yeah, Steve King.'

'At least we have a name,' Erasmus said.

DS Black stepped towards him. 'We have more than that, sir. The woman I talked to said King walked into their Saltburn office this morning and rented a flat in the town. She gave me the address and thinks he's there now.'

Erasmus's heart thumped against his chest. 'Come on,

Teo. We're off to Saltburn.' Then he spoke to Black. 'Did they give you his description?'

She smiled at him. 'It's even better than that.' She got her phone. 'They have CCTV cameras in their office operating all the time. She sent me some clear pictures of King.'

DS Black gave her mobile to Erasmus. He checked the images several times, feeling the heat burning his face.

'What's wrong?' Teo said. 'You look like you've seen a ghost.'

He handed the phone to her. 'Not quite, but that's a dead man's photo.'

Teo scrutinised the image on the screen. 'What do you mean?'

Erasmus tapped the phone to stop his fingers from flexing uncontrollably.

'Steve King is not his real name. That's Steven Cook.'

'Where do I know that name from?' Teo said.

Erasmus took the phone from her and gripped it tightly.

'Steven Cook is Amy Watson's biological father. According to the Ministry of Defence, the man who died in Afghanistan nine years ago.'

Chapter 38

The Friend

Erasmus got Teo to drive, worried his nervous excitement would make him irresponsible behind the wheel.

'How can Steven Cook be alive if the MOD told you he was dead?' she asked.

He stared at the countryside on the way to Saltburn. There were plans to build more houses along the stretch, and he imagined soon it might be impossible to look at the sea unless you were standing on the beach. Or the cliffs.

'They either lied to me or thought it was true,' he said.

'Why would the Ministry of Defence lie to the police?'

Erasmus felt the pill bottle rattling in his jacket pocket. 'I can think of several reasons, but we'll ask Cook when we see him.'

'If he's still there.'

They entered the town and drove past the replica of the pier.

'Let's hope so. Where's the flat?'

She took a left turn. 'It's on Milton Street, near a Chinese Takeaway.'

There was a rumbling in Erasmus's stomach that wasn't from hunger.

'I know where it is. They do a great egg foo young.'

Teo turned right at the end, and Erasmus saw the takeaway. She parked outside and removed her seatbelt, but he didn't move.

'What are you waiting for?' she said.

'You have to buzz the flat to get in.'

Impatience seeped out of her. 'So?'

'If we tell him we're the police, he might do a runner.'

She peered at the flat above the takeaway. 'Is there another way out of there?'

'There'll be plenty of windows to climb out of. He could drop into a neighbouring backyard or an alley before disappearing long before we could catch him.'

'Shall I call for backup?'

Erasmus shook his head. 'No. He might not even be here.'

Teo peered into his eyes. 'You want to lie to him if he answers?'

He shrugged. 'He'll be more trusting if he hears a woman's voice, but not if you think it means doing anything unethical.'

She stepped out of the car. 'Just get on with it, Erasmus.'

He removed his seatbelt, followed her and pressed the buzzer for the flat, and they waited. Thirty seconds later, they got a response.

'Who is it?'

'I'm from the housing association, Mr King. We forgot an important piece of paper we need you to sign.'

Erasmus expected a protest but heard a click to open the door. He moved inside quickly, and they climbed the stairs two at a time. Teo knocked on the entrance to the flat when they got there. The sound of feet shuffling put Erasmus on edge, and he held his breath. When the door opened, he gazed into a dead man's eyes. His warrant card was open and in his hand.

'We need to speak to you about Jack Trent, Mr King.'

The dead man glanced between them both before his shoulders slumped.

'You better come in, then.'

Erasmus let Teo enter before closing the door and watching the resurrected Steven Cook follow her into the living room. He scanned the place, which was sparsely furnished with a small sofa, flat-screen TV, and a coffee table.

Teo had a notebook in one hand and a pen in the other. 'Were you friends with Jack Trent, Mr King?'

He didn't answer the question. 'Has something happened to him?'

Erasmus scrutinised his face. The death on the train tracks had featured in the media, but the police hadn't released Trent's name or mentioned it as murder. Several websites had commented on those things, but the man in front of them may not have seen those posts. So maybe he didn't know Trent's fate.

'He's dead, Steven,' Erasmus said. 'We thought you might help us understand why somebody would want to kill him.'

The man with the fake surname put his hands to his face and sank onto the sofa. He was a big bloke, over six feet tall, with a bodybuilder's physique, so he made a hefty sound when he slumped into the seat. He sat quietly for a minute before removing his hands and staring at Erasmus.

'You know my name isn't Steve King, right?'

Erasmus nodded. 'Do you know what happened to your daughter, Mr Cook?'

Cook dug into his pocket and removed a mobile phone.

'Sure,' he said and gave the device to Erasmus.

Erasmus gazed at the screen, his legs wavering as he watched an animated Amy Watson sitting on a golden beach making sandcastles. He put one hand on the wall to steady himself and struggled to breathe. When he finally calmed the thunder in his chest, he passed the phone to Teo. He couldn't speak, so she did.

'When was this taken, Steve?'

Cook wiped something away from under his eye. 'Two weeks ago, in Majorca.'

As relief swept through him, Erasmus controlled the urge to shout.

'Jack Trent helped you kidnap Amy last year.'

Cook slammed his fist into his leg. 'She wasn't kidnapped. Amy wanted to come with me. I didn't force her to do anything.' He snarled at Erasmus. 'Look at how happy she is in that video.'

Teo stepped between the two men. 'Start from the beginning, Steve. Tell us everything.'

Erasmus was standing behind her, so she obscured him from Cook. He slipped his phone into his pocket, setting the video to record. Then he moved to the side so he could see Cook speak.

'I met Jack when we were fourteen. Our parents were on holiday in Crete, and we were the only two teenagers there. We bonded over Suede and Nirvana, plus our common dislike for London football clubs. He loved the Boro, and I'm an Aston Villa fan.' He rolled up his shirt-sleeve to show the tattoo of the club badge. 'We kept in touch, and he'd often stay with me in Birmingham, going to gigs and the football. Then, when I joined the army, I'd always stay over in Teesside with him and his parents when I was on leave. That's how I knew so much about the area and could sweet talk Jane when I bumped into her in Cyprus.'

'Amy's mother,' Teo said.

'It was a brief holiday fling for both of us. At least, that's what I thought. I only found out years later she'd had a baby. Jack recognised her from the estate and told me in his letters.'

Erasmus never took his eyes off him. 'This was after you'd supposedly died in Afghanistan?'

'Have you heard of The Increment?' Cook asked.

Erasmus shook his head. 'Is it a special ops group?'

Cook nodded. 'The Increment or E Squadron undertakes sanctioned high-value targeting and other hazardous tasks. Whilst technically a Special Forces unit underneath SAS, The Increment accepts assignments directly from UK Intelligence agencies such as MI6. Therefore, the unit functions semi-autonomously from the rest of the UK Special Forces.'

'And you were part of this squadron?'

'I was for five years. Then, when the Royal Military Police began investigating suspected British military war crimes in Afghanistan, it became prudent for my superiors to "retire" me and several others. That's why the MOD told you I was dead.'

He peered deep into Cook's eyes and knew he wasn't lying. 'Why take Amy from her mother and stepfather?'

Cook shook his head. 'You know why. Jack knew I was alive, and we kept in touch. He told me how that cow was neglecting Amy.' He turned both hands into fists. 'And how that bastard Robinson would hurt her. I wouldn't let my daughter stay in that environment. And since I was offi-cially dead, I couldn't come back here for her. So, I got Jack to contact Amy and tell her about me. Then we spoke and had video chats using Jack's phone. Any normal mother should have known what was happening with her eight-year-old kid, but Jane was too busy shooting up with her druggie sister.'

'How did you get her away from Teesside?' Teo said.

Erasmus replied before Cook did. 'You couldn't use the roads or trains because Amy's picture was plastered all over the media. So, you got Trent as a Border Force officer to sneak her out of the country through the port?'

Cook laughed. 'You'd be amazed how much goes in and out of that Freeport that shouldn't. Everything worked perfectly, and Amy came to live with my girlfriend and me in Majorca. And do you know what?' He leaned forward, and Erasmus saw the muscles ripple beneath his shirt. 'She's never asked about her mother once in twelve months. Soon, the scars on her back should be fully healed.'

Erasmus felt his phone humming in his pocket. 'So why did you return to Teesside?'

'Jack needed a favour, and I couldn't turn him down after he'd helped me so much.'

'What favour?' Teo said.

'He was scared,' Cook answered. 'What he'd done to get Amy out of the country was behind his boss's back. And I don't mean the Border Force people – I'm talking about the criminals he worked for. Helping Amy – helping me – placed Jack in danger. So, I came back to help him.' He put his head in his hands again. 'But it looks like I was too late.'

'Do you know the name of the person Jack worked for in this organised crime gang?' Erasmus said.

Cook removed his hands. 'No, he wouldn't tell me until

I got here and we met. But he had evidence against this gang: videos of what they do.'

Erasmus nearly fell over. 'Where is this evidence?'

Cook shrugged. 'Did you check his home?'

'We did,' Teo said. 'There was nothing there.'

'I can only think of one other place,' Cook replied.

Erasmus moved forward and loomed over him. 'Where?'

Steel possessed Cook's face. 'What happens to Amy now?'

Erasmus got his phone and stopped the recording. 'She has to come back here, Steve, you know that. But I promise to get you the best legal aid regarding her custody.'

'What about his fake death?' Teo said.

'I'm sure the MOD and the British government will look after one of their decorated officers. What do you think, Steve?'

'I guess,' Cook replied. 'And you'll help me with a solicitor and Amy?'

Erasmus nodded. 'I give you my word. Call your girlfriend and tell her to take Amy to the nearest police station.' He faced Teo. 'Contact the Majorcan authorities and inform them about what's happening.'

He watched them making their phone calls, hoping the broken window that was his heart might finally be fixed.

Chapter 39

The Evidence

As Erasmus called Beckett, Cook sat in the back of the car and gave Teo directions.

'Amy Watson is alive?' the chief inspector said.

'Yes. Teo spoke to the Majorcan police, who will take care of her and contact the British Embassy. You need to send somebody to inform her mother, Sam. But it's probably best not to give her or the stepfather too many details and definitely don't mention the resurrected Steven Cook.'

'Are you bringing him here?' Beckett asked.

He glanced at Amy's father in the rear-view mirror. 'Soon. We're headed to Jack Trent's parent's house to look for this evidence Cook mentioned. You should tell the MOD about him as well.'

'Okay, Erasmus. I'll speak to you again at the station.'

He ended the call as they pulled onto the street. 'It's the one at the end,' Cook said, 'with the purple door.'

She drove past the bank and the bicycle shop where Erasmus always got his bikes fixed, found a spot a few doors away and parked.

'Stay here with him,' Erasmus said. 'I shouldn't be long.'

She grabbed his arm before he could get out of the car. 'I'll come with you.'

He leaned into her. 'No. I need you to make sure he doesn't leave.'

She laughed. 'Have you seen the size of him? He could eat me for breakfast.'

Erasmus grinned at her. 'You're a resourceful woman, DS Andreescu. You'll think of something if you have to.'

He exited the car quickly so he couldn't hear her protests. Then he rushed to the house, raising his hand to knock on the door when he noticed it was ajar. He pushed it open and stepped inside.

'Hello, Mr and Mrs Trent. Are you home?'

It was a small, terraced house with a narrow corridor leading into the living room. Erasmus entered and saw the place in disarray: somebody had used a knife to tear the sofa apart, with its guts thrown all over the carpet. A table was upturned on its side, with magazines scattered everywhere. Near the window were broken pieces of porcelain figures and teacups.

He felt into his pocket for his mobile when he heard the whimpering from upstairs. Erasmus moved to the stairs and climbed slowly. He didn't call out, brushing past the photos on the wall of a young Jack Trent. A teenage Steven Cook was also in some of the pictures.

Erasmus reached the top, hearing the crying in the nearest bedroom. He went to the doorway and stopped, frozen by the sight of an elderly man lying on the floor. Then he saw David Miller standing over a woman as she lay on the bed. He had a large kitchen knife at her throat.

'What a surprise, the pigs have arrived.'

'Put the weapon down, David, before you get into even more trouble.'

Miller grinned at him. 'Who says I'm in trouble, copper?'

'You might be good at playing other people's music, but you can't talk your way out of this one.' Erasmus nodded to the man on the carpet. 'Breaking and entering, assault with a deadly weapon, and threatening behaviour. So that's three charges off the top of my head.'

The bloke with the eyepatch continued to smile. 'There'll be more coming off the top of your head in a second.'

Erasmus heard the footsteps behind him too late. George Miller struck him in the face with a large frying pan as he turned. He smelt bacon fat as agony shot through his forehead, putting his arm up as his legs gave way and crashed next to the man he assumed was Jack Trent's father on the carpet. His hip hit the skirting board, and he groaned.

'What are we going to do with him, Davey?' George Miller said.

His brother moved away from the whimpering Mrs Trent.

'We'll do nowt. He can stay here with the other two. He's got no proof we were here – it would only be his word against ours. And there are plenty of people to give us alibis.' David stepped over Erasmus. 'Did you find the stuff downstairs?'

George shook his head. 'No. It must be up here.'

Erasmus rolled onto his back and stared at them. 'It's hard to tell which of you is the stupidest, since you're both such idiots.'

David Miller waved the blade close to Erasmus's face. 'What makes you think I won't just gut you now?'

Erasmus laughed. 'Okay. The pirate is the stupid one.'

He thrust his hand forward and grabbed the knife. It sliced into his palm, and a burning agony sped through him. He jumped to his feet as his blood dripped onto the carpet. The Miller brothers were slow of thought and action, standing open-mouthed as Erasmus punched David in the face and the knife dropped to the floor. Then he turned and threw himself at George. He crashed into the younger brother, and they tumbled out of the room together, hitting the landing before rolling down the stairs. He ended up on top of George, his lungs feeling as if they were full of water. He ached everywhere and readied himself for another attack until he saw Miller was out cold.

'Is this why you didn't want me in the house?' Teo said from the doorway. 'So you could play at wrestling with the hospital porter?'

Erasmus rolled away and rested against the wall. 'The other one is upstairs with the Trents, who I think these bastards have hurt.'

She waved her phone at him. 'I've already called for reinforcements and an ambulance.'

He watched her walk upstairs as he put a bloodied hand on his leg. He didn't worry about her going up there alone.

If David Miller was still conscious, he was the one Erasmus was worried about.

Chapter 40

The Port

Erasmus flexed his bandaged fingers as he and Teo stood with a group of Border Force officers at the port and watched a ship being loaded with containers for export.

'How's the hand?' she asked.

He grimaced. 'It stings, but it's nothing a few drinks won't fix later.'

'Are you going to the airport to meet Amy off the plane?'

Erasmus smiled, still finding it hard to believe Amy Watson was alive and returning to Teesside.

'I told her father I would. My contact at social services will ensure Jane Watson and Billy Robinson can't get custody of her until we sort this whole mess out.'

He stared at a large container hanging in the air as it was lowered onto a ship.

'Speaking of which,' Teo said. 'What was happening with Steven Cook? I didn't see him again after we took him to the station.'

'Beckett's dealing with all of that. He told me somebody from the MOD was hot-footing their way there as we left.

Regardless of his involvement in smuggling Amy out of the country, Cook has some kudos going for him for leading us to those hard drives in the Trent family house.'

Teo laughed. 'How stupid are those Miller brothers? They should have looked under the bed first, not last.'

Erasmus grinned. The cybercrime officers hadn't had the opportunity to go through everything on the six hard drives they'd found, but they'd seen enough to put Alex West and his gang behind bars for a long time. And it would stop the import of illegal drugs into the country for a bit. But only for a short while. He knew others would take West's place and find another UK port to bribe their way through. It didn't matter how many organised crime gangs the police stopped; there would always be more to replace them.

'Do you think we'll find a video of Jack Trent's murder?'

She shrugged. 'If not, one of the gang will spill their guts to get a deal.'

Erasmus wasn't too sure. 'I guess so.'

The noise from the containers loaded onto the ship increased, and Teo grimaced. 'How long do you want to stay here?'

'Not long,' he said.

They'd gone there as part of a team, arresting two Border Force employees and a member of staff working for the Freeport. So, it wouldn't surprise him if, after his colleagues had forensically checked those hard drives, they'd return to the port for more arrests.

'Good,' she said. 'I need a drink, and you're buying.'

He moved closer to the man overseeing the loading. 'Where are those going?' Erasmus asked.

'China,' the official replied. 'Machinery and transport equipment.'

They observed the operation, noticing a significant difference between it and the checks on goods coming into the port.

'How come fewer people scrutinise exports compared to imports?'

The man shrugged. 'The Chinese companies have long-standing relationships with us, so there's no need for as much red tape. And it's one of the benefits of the Freeports.'

Erasmus watched as people checked the paperwork for the exports, but nobody opened any containers.

'You don't check what's inside them?'

The man shook his head. 'We might for one or two. We don't have the time or the staff to look into all of them. Honestly, since it's goods leaving the country, the powers that be don't really care.'

No wonder nobody noticed Trent smuggling Amy out of the country.

He left them to work, and Erasmus pulled Teo to the side.

'West wasn't only smuggling drugs into the UK from East Asia. He's been sneaking something out.'

'What?'

He observed the large-scale operation going on around them and wondered.

'I don't know.'

She puffed out her cheeks. 'Could he have been trafficking drugs out of the country as well?'

The pain in Erasmus's hand increased, with a second front opening at the back of his skull. Before he could answer, Jesse Sullivan stepped out of the Border Force office and joined them.

'I still can't believe Jack would do that.'

Erasmus noticed her lips trembling and wondered if something had happened between her and Trent.

'None of us can ever know what's inside another person's mind,' he said.

He thought of his father rotting beneath those bushes for five years, lying undiscovered as people walked past him only a few feet away. Then he pictured his mother in the care home, surrounded by others but still on her own.

Sullivan continued. 'But Jack had so much potential, more than anybody else who works here. He was clever. Really clever. He could have done anything but this: lawyer, scientist, even a doctor.'

'Doctor?' Erasmus said.

She wiped a tear from her eye. 'For sure. I told him it wasn't too late to go to university, to get a degree.' She took a deep breath. 'I thought I'd got through to him when he started bringing medical books and journals here to read during his breaks. The other staff would mess around on their phones, playing games or watching daft videos, but Jack would have his head stuck in his books.'

Erasmus stared at her. 'You saw him doing this?'

Sullivan nodded. 'All the time. Once, I noticed him on his work computer looking at one of those torsos that shows you all the organs inside the human body. I assumed he was going to buy it for his studies.' She shrugged. 'But I don't think he ever did.' She looked at Erasmus. 'Did you find one of those at his place?'

He shook his head. 'No.'

Sullivan replaced a stray hair behind her ear. 'Ah well, I guess you're right - we can never know what's in another person's thoughts, no matter how well we think we know them.'

Erasmus nodded. 'The enigma of the human mind.'

He watched her return to the office as his vision changed to something he'd seen before but forgotten.

'I love you,' his father had said.

But those words hadn't been for Erasmus.

Never for Erasmus.

Nor were they for his mother.

He tapped Teo on the shoulder. 'I have to go into Middlesbrough. I'll see you back at the station.'

'Do you want a lift?'

He smiled at her. 'I need the exercise.'

Then he headed for the port exit.

Chapter 41

The Resolution

The temperature in the mortuary chilled Erasmus's skin. The smell of antiseptic was mixed with something unexpected: jasmine.

Perfume.

It didn't come from the young woman lying on the table before him. Her chest had been spread open, so he saw a mass of internal organs and inhaled the aroma of blood and sinew. No, the jasmine was drifting from the other person in the room, the one eating the sandwich as she peered into the dead.

'It's grilled ham and cheese,' Dr Bella Toon said. 'From a wonderful place on Linthorpe Road. The only problem is that it's always cold when I get here.' She smiled at him. 'Still, there are worse things in life, aren't there, Erasmus?' She glanced at his bandaged hand. 'Did you have an accident?'

'It's nothing. Don't you ever get a day off, Bella?'

She licked a pickle from the top of her lip. 'You know how it is, my friend.' She dropped the wrapper into the bin. 'So, for what do I owe the pleasure of this unexpected visit?'

He moved closer to the corpse. 'My curiosity has been nagging at me.'

She smiled at him. 'You better be careful, Erasmus – look what curiosity did to that cat.'

'Weren't they a terrible pop group from the 80s?'

Bella laughed. 'Indeed. I always forget we have the same taste in music. Do you still listen to The Smiths under cover of darkness?'

He glanced at the open chest near him, thinking he saw something move inside it.

'Nothing lies more convincingly than nostalgia.'

She moved from him to a sink and washed her hands. Then she slipped on a pair of plastic gloves. 'Have you had a break in the Jack Trent murder?'

He watched her remove the organs and place them in separate containers.

'Haven't you heard?' he said.

'I've been stuck in here all day. Who would have thought there would be so many people off sick in a hospital?'

'We shut down a major organised crime gang this morning, the ones who had Trent killed. It's one of the reasons I'm here.'

'Congratulations, Erasmus. That is good news.'

He glanced away from what he imagined was wriggling in the blood.

'It is, but unfortunately for the hospital, one of the staff was a member of this criminal organisation.'

Bella peered at him. 'Somebody from here?'

'Yes, a porter – George Miller. Do you know him?'

She shook her head. 'No, I don't think so. This place must employ hundreds of people.'

Erasmus got his phone and showed her a photo of Miller. 'You've never seen him?'

Bella narrowed her eyes. 'I might have, of course. It would be easy to walk past somebody here and not notice them.'

'He never came to the mortuary or brought and removed bodies from here?'

'I don't know, Erasmus. You'd have to check his work record.'

'We will.'

'What's this about?' she asked.

He put his phone away. 'A local businessman, Alex West, ran this organised crime gang that George Miller worked for. Have you heard of him?'

'I can't say I have. Outside this place and my family, I see little of Teesside. So what did these criminals do?'

'They mainly imported Class A drugs from East Asia: heroin and cocaine. But I think they might have had another side-line.'

'And what was that?'

'Selling human organs for illegal transplants.'

Bella laughed. 'Really?'

Erasmus nodded. 'On my first day back at work, I saw a couple fighting at the station. She needed a kidney transplant, and the NHS waiting list was full for the next three years. Her husband convinced her he could find somebody to help her if she gave him £5,000, which she did. And then he lost it all on the horses.'

Bella shook her head. 'Five grand wouldn't have got her a healthy kidney.'

'How much would it cost?'

She shrugged. 'I'm unsure – maybe twenty times that.'

'Wow!' Erasmus said. 'No wonder there's a black market in organ trafficking.'

'Wait – you think the hospital porter was stealing organs for this organised crime gang?'

The wound in his hand throbbed. 'Would it be possible?'

Bella puffed out her cheeks. 'Well, there would be several issues to consider, procurement and transportation being the main two.'

'Could he have got around those?'

'I doubt it. Maybe twenty years ago, but not now. Until an inquiry in 1999, the public was unaware that hospitals within the NHS were keeping patients' organs without family consent.'

Erasmus rubbed at his bandage. 'I remember that in the news at the time.'

'It was all over the media,' Bella said. 'The Alder Hey organs scandal involved the unauthorised removal, retention, and disposal of human tissue, including children's organs, from 1988 to 1996. During this period, the hospital kept organs in over two thousand pots containing body parts from around eight hundred and fifty infants. These were later uncovered at Alder Hey Children's Hospital, Liverpool, during a public inquiry into the scandal. This led to the Human Tissue Act 2004, overhauling legislation regarding handling human tissues in the UK and creating the Human Tissue Authority. The Human Tissue Act prohibits the selling of organs. In addition, the HTA regulates the removal, storage, use and disposal of human bodies, organs and tissue for several scheduled purposes, such as research, transplantation, education and training. The Act makes consent the fundamental principle underpinning the lawful storage and use of body parts, organs and tissue from the living or the deceased for specified health-related purposes and public display.'

'Okay, Bella, that covers all the legal requirements, but could organs be illegally removed from this hospital with no one knowing?'

'You mean after a post-mortem?'

'I do.'

She took a few seconds to think about it. 'Following the examination, the organs are returned to the body minus the pieces preserved for future work or evidence or cremated, in accordance with the law and the family's wishes. The breastbone and ribs are also usually put back. So, to answer your question, the only way to achieve it would be with the help of somebody in the mortuary.'

'That's what I thought,' he said.

Bella's eyes darkened. 'Is this porter claiming to have removed organs from the hospital?'

He flexed his fingers, but the pain didn't disappear. 'Not yet.'

'Why would any forensic pathologist do such a thing, Erasmus? The financial rewards wouldn't outweigh the risk to their career, reputation, or freedom.'

'A hundred grand for each kidney? You'd only have to misplace two or three a year to have a nice pension to look forward to.'

'*Me?*'

He laughed. 'I was speaking theoretically. It's one of those curious things I said that brought me here.'

'Your curiosity?'

Erasmus nodded. 'How you discovered Trent had died through choking on a small crab, considering his body was in pieces after being hit by the train, was pure brilliance, Bella.'

She grinned. 'What can I say? I'm smarter than the average forensic pathologist.'

'Yes, my father always said that about you, how you were the cleverest student at medical school.'

Bella touched the torso. 'I wouldn't have got where I am today without James's help.'

Erasmus touched his chin. 'And that's one of the things that irked my curiosity. How could you deduce what killed Jack Trent from such meagre pickings, yet couldn't say for definite if somebody had struck my father on the head or if he died from a fall?'

'I don't want to sound harsh, Erasmus, but when your colleagues brought your father's remains to me, there wasn't much left but bones. And after five years, it would always be difficult to say precisely how he died.'

'How old were you when you met my father, Bella?'

She removed her bloodied gloves and threw them into a bin.

'It was when I joined medical school, so I would have been eighteen.'

'And he was more than twice your age?'

She strode around the corpse. 'Organ trafficking and now this. What are you getting at?'

'How soon after meeting my father did you sleep with him?'

Her face froze, mimicking the dead woman on the table. And then she laughed.

'Are you having one of your episodes, Erasmus? Perhaps you need to return to Redlands. Would you like me to organise an ambulance to take you there?'

'It went on for over two decades, didn't it? Even after you were married and had kids, you continued having an affair with my father.' She didn't reply. 'You know, I saw the two of you together once here, in the hospital. At the time, I thought it was one of my hallucinations and pushed it to the back of my mind. It wasn't long before he disappeared. He told you he loved you, but you said you'd never loved him. I remember it clearly now.'

She smiled at him. 'So, I'm an organ trafficker, adulterer, and what? A murderer?'

'I don't have any evidence of this, Bella. And if any of your DNA were still clinging to my father's bones, I guess you'd have got rid of it during the post-mortem. I just need to know I'm not losing my mind again.'

'Show me your phone, Erasmus,' she said. He placed it on the table next to the body. Then she went to him and ran her fingers over his chest, arms, and legs. 'Just to be sure.'

'You think I came here to record a confession secretly?'

She touched his cheek. 'We're the same age, Erasmus. How come we never got together?'

Her touch was both warm and cold. 'You were married when I first met you.'

She pushed back her head and laughed. 'Ah yes, my dear husband, Brian. He is a crashing bore both in and out of the bedroom.' She stroked his fingers. 'I should have seduced you like I did your father to keep it in the family.' She grinned as she spoke. 'Perhaps then he wouldn't have pestered me so much in the end.'

'Pestered you?'

Bella removed her fingers from his. 'Once he knew your mother was going into the care home, he thought we could finally be together and let the world know.'

'Your kids are grown up, so you could have left your husband, the man you hate.'

'I don't hate anybody, Erasmus. I abhor boredom, and your father took me away from that. He had a very open mind where sex was concerned.' She glanced around the mortuary. 'We did it here a few times, right next to the dead.' Her laugh made the hairs on his neck stand up. 'He enjoyed the danger nearly as much as I did, that excitement from knowing you could be caught at any time. That's why he couldn't get enough of sex in public places.'

Erasmus pictured his adulterous father running like a sex-obsessed Heathcliff towards his doom. 'It was you who got him to the cliffs.'

'I told him it was over, but he wouldn't listen and threatened to tell my husband everything unless I stayed with him.'

'Why did you care what Brian thought?'

She shrugged. 'I didn't, but James said he'd also go to the hospital board and tell them what we'd done in this room. I'd have lost my job instantly and wasn't prepared for that. I've worked too hard to get here to let some foolish old man threaten what I've achieved.'

Erasmus took a deep breath. 'So you killed him?'

Bella looked mortified. 'No. We fucked in that dirty, smelly fanhouse, and I told him that was it. So I left, and he ran after me. That's when he tripped and hit his head on a rock.'

He peered into her eyes, unsure if she was telling the truth. 'Why didn't you call for an ambulance?'

'I checked, Erasmus. Your father was already dead.'

'So why leave him like that, rotting beneath the bushes for five years?'

'And how would I explain what we'd done out there? The hospital would have sacked me on the spot. No, I covered him and left the rest to nature. It was no worse than being stuck in a box six feet under or burnt to a crisp.'

'Or maybe you killed him and dumped him there.'

She shook her head. 'It was an accident.'

'When did you meet Alex West?'

Bella stepped away from him and returned to the corpse. She grabbed a saucer containing one of the dead woman's organs.

'Are we back to illegal organ trafficking?' The blood swished around in the dish. 'Do you think I'd trust a lowly hospital porter to help me if I was involved in that?'

'So, in theory, how would it be done?'

She raised the dish as if getting ready to toss pizza dough in the air.

'In theory, Erasmus, it would be so simple.' She put the dish next to the dead woman. 'This kidney can remain viable outside the body for twenty-four to thirty-six hours under the proper conditions. And anybody can buy an organ transport box online.'

'So, you'd stitch the body back together, falsify the paperwork regarding what organs you'd returned to the body, and then place the stolen organ in one of these transport boxes?'

'No, Erasmus, *I* wouldn't do any of those things. But a criminal medical professional might.'

He nodded. 'Then how would they get the box out of the hospital without being seen?'

She removed her gown and walked to where her coat was hanging. Then she reached down and lifted a large sports bag.

'I sometimes go for a game of tennis straight from here. These bags are big enough to carry a lot of things.'

'The tennis club. Is that where you met Alex West?'

Her face darkened. 'Okay, Erasmus, I've had enough of your games. You should go home and celebrate the success of solving your investigation. What happened with your father was unfortunate, but it's all in the past. So, you should move forward and get on with your life. Like I will.'

He peered beyond her. 'You can come in now.'

DCI Brennan strode in, followed by Teo and two uniformed officers.

Dr Bella Toon didn't seem phased. 'More games, Erasmus?'

He lifted his bandaged hand and pointed at the screen in the corner, the one used for viewing post-mortems from outside the mortuary.

She clutched the sports bag. 'I turned that off well before you arrived.'

Teo grinned at her. 'And we switched it back on before Erasmus came in here.'

Bella glanced at the screen. 'The light would have come on.'

DCI Brennan strode forward. 'Oh, we got one of our tech guys to disable that but still have the recording equipment work.'

Erasmus watched Bella's face turn darker than her heart, hearing Brennan tell Dr Toon she had the right to remain silent.

Chapter 42

The Walk

Erasmus's legs throbbed as he gazed across the cliffs at Saltburn pier cutting into the sea.

'I hope you brought a water bottle,' Teo said at his side.

He wiped the sweat from his forehead. 'I told you – we're going to my favourite pub in Loftus. They do the best gin and tonics in the county.'

She stared at the panoramic view of the town. 'It's glorious up here.'

Erasmus held out his bandaged hand. 'And there's only a gentle breeze to push us on our way.'

Teo's phone pinged, and she checked the message. 'My mother wants me to come and visit her in Whitby.'

He nodded. 'Is this because you gave her that money?'

'I leant her the cash but, probably, yes.'

'Why don't you go? It's prettier than sulking in Middlesbrough.'

She scowled at him. 'Who says I'm sulking?'

The wind disturbed his hair as he laughed. 'Your face does, for one.'

Teo punched him in the arm, and he released a fake cry of pain.

'Why would I be sulking?'

He flexed his fingers. 'Because I think you're lonely.'

Erasmus thought she'd punch him again, only for real this time, but she didn't.

'How can I be lonely when I have you as a friend?'

He laughed. 'How true.'

'So, are we reversing the route we took the other day – going from here to Skinningrove and then up to Loftus?'

'That we are, Teo.'

'Okay, so what are we waiting for?'

'You mean, who are we waiting for?'

Confusion spread over her face. 'What?'

He pointed at the small cottages and the people coming across from the path.

'I thought we might need a musical accompaniment as we walked.'

He watched her eyes sparkle as Sapphy and the rest of the Hex Pistols ran to them.

Alma got there first. 'I'm so glad you agreed to this, Teo.'

Teo shrugged. 'I enjoy walking, and the scenery is spectacular here.'

'She doesn't mean that,' Sapphy said. 'We're happy you let Erasmus convince you to be in our music video.'

Teo bit her top lip. 'Wait, what?'

The four Hex Pistols thrust their phones into Teo's face and started filming. Erasmus grinned as he grabbed her arm and pulled Teo up the path and away from the cliff's edge.

'Don't worry, DS Andreescu – you can always arrest them if you don't like the footage.'

She laughed with him as they set off on the walk,

watching the others recording everything and anything. They walked for two minutes before she spoke to him again.

'What you did, Erasmus, finding Amy Watson after she'd been missing for over a year is nothing short of a miracle.'

He smiled at her. 'We did it together, Teo.'

She returned his smile. 'Yeah, of course, but it was remarkable, don't you think?'

He guessed what was on her mind. 'It was, and it taught us all a valuable lesson.'

'What was that?' she asked.

He glanced at the ocean below them.

'Never give up hope. What once was lost can always be found again.'

Thank You!

Thank you, dear reader for purchasing this book.

Many thanks to my wonderful wife for all her support and patience.

Extra special thanks to Karina Gallagher for being a dedicated reader of my work.

Cover design by James, GoOnWrite.com

Mailing List & Free Books!

If you would like to join my mailing list and receive a free eBook then contact me at <u>mail@andrewsfrench.com</u>

About the Author

Andrew French lives amongst faded seaside glamour on the North East coast of England. He likes gin and cats but not together, new music and old movies, curry and ice cream. Slow bike rides and long walks to the pub are his usual exercise, as well as flicking through the pages of good books and the memoirs of bad people.

Find out more at www.andrewsfrench.com

Facebook:

https://www.facebook.com/A-S-French-Author-150145625006018

Twitter:

www.twitter.com/andrewfrench100

Instagram:

www.instagram.com/andrewfrench100

And replies to all his email at mail@andrewsfrench.com

If you have the time, please leave a review at Amazon or Goodreads

Thank you!

www.ingramcontent.com/pod-product-compliance
Lightning Source LLC
Chambersburg PA
CBHW011552190726
48287CB00010B/2851